# CASCADE

GREAT PLACE BOOKS

**Julia Hannafin**

# CASCADE

PUBLISHED BY GREAT PLACE BOOKS
WWW.GREATPLACEBOOKS.COM
COPYRIGHT © 2024 JULIA HANNAFIN
ALL RIGHTS RESERVED

DESCRIPTION: FIRST EDITION
PUBLISHER NAME: GREAT PLACE BOOKS
CITY OF PUBLICATION: CHICAGO, ILLINOIS
AUTHOR: JULIA HANNAFIN
LCCN: 2024930614
ISBN: 978-1-950987-58-0
DESIGNED BY AIDAN FITZGERALD
GPB 02

*For Dawn*

There is a starfish that sees with the surface of its body. The brittle star doesn't have eyes defined by little globes cased in eyelids—its whole body sees. To see itself, then, is just to interact with the world, to move through it. I wish I could live this way.

The boat rocks up and down. I slide from white plastic seat to boat floor, where I grip the metal above me, staring through the railing into the ocean. The water makes infinite patterns, waves, impossibly coordinated lines of blue, gray, white, and brown.

I can still see Erin standing in the kitchen, frozen, her arm bent, her hand holding her cell phone inches away from her ear. She couldn't say anything to me at first. The house was quiet, still, all music subtracted. I was supposed to go to college and med school, to become a surgeon so I could pick things apart with steady hands. Blake wanted it for me as badly as I wanted it for myself. When Blake died, I couldn't keep walking in the direction that kept me on her map. I had to go somewhere else.

On the boat Michael's face suddenly looms over me, concerned,

dirty blonde hair going wild past the edges of his hat, and I immediately see my ex-boyfriend Julian's face in his—the sharp, dark eyes,
the long eyelashes, the gap between the two front teeth—before
I notice the wrinkles that crease out to his temples, the crooked
(maybe broken?) nose, the sun damaged skin. It's like I can see how
Julian's going to age, his body fast-forwarded into the future,
standing in front of me.

Twenty-seven miles didn't sound like too many. My ears start
to heat up, my nose dripping down my chin. Michael reaches for
the straps of my lifejacket and tugs, testing their tightness. He
yanks the carabiner that's attached to my middle, that runs a line
from me to the boat so I don't go overboard. "Are you good?" He
yells over the wind and the engine.

Our destination is the Farallon Islands, twenty-seven miles
past San Francisco. You can see them on a clear day from Berkeley,
all their islands making one crunchy line on the horizon. Erin
used to think it was good luck, spotting them, proof of the universe's benevolent will.

"I promised I'd take care of you," Michael says.

I first met Michael when I picked Julian up from his house in
the Oakland hills and he invited me inside. The house was nice,
a Craftsman perched atop too many stairs. Strange sculptures in
the corners, brightly colored lumps of clay. There were framed
photos of water on the walls. On the fridge, some of family.
We sat in the den, where Julian and his dad traded off inserting
records into the record player—wandering into the corner, lining
up the grooves, then muttering a few words about what they'd

like to put on next. Michael assembled a cheese plate. I didn't eat anything until he nudged a plate toward me again and said they're from the Cheeseboard, "You have to try one." Julian wanted to drink a beer, but his dad gave him a look: "Keep it outside the house."

Berkeley parents were often like this—cultured, smart, interesting, self-pronounced weirdos with beautiful houses—but I'd never believed in them fully. The dads were too self-referential. They read the news too much and they wanted to teach you about Roman history or sustainable fruit farming. Michael was different. I wanted to hear everything about his life and what he thought of the world—I'd touch all the details of his house and ask about them so I could prompt him to keep talking. I complimented the water portraits and found out Michael was a scientist and a researcher. "Worked with the water a long timehe said, as if the ocean were a colleague. Julian scowled.

I ate another piece of cheese mashed into a cracker. Grease gathered in shiny circles on my fingertips. I learned that Michael studied marine mammals and I asked more questions. Where have you gone for work? What's the biggest animal you've ever gotten close to? The sun sank through the windows and into his arms, the body hairs bleached blonde from all the time in the field.

"You go for the males when they're sleeping—" Michael told me and Julian. He was describing the summer he first tagged elephant seals. It was clearly a story Julian had heard before, but I didn't care that Julian didn't care. "—The females notice you right away, barking and shrieking, but the males don't wake up. You sneak up to the dozing male, take his flippers in your hands, spread them to find the webbing. Find your courage and—staple the tag down between the fingers and then get the fuck out of there, because they'll spring right back and bite your fucking hand off."

My moms never swore when I was growing up. I thought about being Julian, listening to this story the first time Michael told it, excising my boyfriend from the space next to me. I exhaled, "Fuck," and laughed, because that's what felt natural, using his language, not mine, like I was sitting in a sports bar with this man, the only girl in a crowd of guys, my elbows on the counter. I uncrossed my legs, let my knees float outward, and my voice slowed and deepened. Julian, not yet erasable, watched me closely.

Michael studied elephant seals when he was younger, but around the time Julian was born, he switched his focus to great white sharks. He's been running a long-term study of individual great white sharks, tagging, photographing, and counting the sharks that pass through the Farallons and feed every fall and winter. "It's actually less dangerous than working with elephant seals," he said, but I didn't believe him. He squeezed his hands, smiling, enjoying telling me this story. I leaned in, wanting more. Julian got restless and, tugging at me, told his dad we had to go.

Julian was supposed to go on this trip, this boat, not me, but he got pneumonia and had to drop out. I turn away from Michael's face, back to the water. I'm hidden at the front of the boat, which all the men onboard warned me was worst for seasickness. The bow makes consistent waves that spread and foam at the boat's sides; a jellyfish appears for a few seconds before the wake disappears it. Its top is large and circular, a see-through brain with orange squiggles, and it drags behind long yellow tentacles three times the size of its head.

"You might be more comfortable inside the cabin," he tells me, but I want to stay where I can see where we're going.

Our boat is large and sturdy, made of steel. In decaying red paint along the side, there's a woman's name: MARIANNE. Marianne's front is curved, and her back is squared off with another boat on top of it. I've been told this is a two-part trip: first on the big boat, then on the small. The man driving the big boat is a volunteer. He has a friendly face and a faded neck tattoo of a vine. He will leave us on the islands and come back with supplies in a few weeks.

When I took his place, Julian was surprised that I wanted the job—he told me the work is long and slow. "You don't get answers right away," he warned me. "It storms that time of year. It's hard work." He was being condescending, but the description also sent adrenaline up the back of my neck.

"I'll stay at the front of the boat," I tell Michael. "I'm good, thanks."

There hasn't been land in hours. My hair blows away from my face and I turn toward where the rolling hills of Pt. Reyes should be, continuing on our right far longer than San Francisco on our left, but now it's only fog, a gray-white mass which splits occasionally, the layers thinning to reveal the horizon line, water forever.

When I researched what the boat ride would be like, I kept reading: "washing machine." There was a report of a racing sailboat that crashed when it came around the corner of the southeastern island and was toppled by a huge wave. The water is still and the foam constant and a wave comes out of nowhere, bigger than I imagined possible, and the boat goes up and down, hard. Side to side, hard. Then it's calm again. My stomach has to catch up.

There is water along my hairline and I don't know if it's spray or sweat, because I feel hot and very cold. My chest tries to crunch down so it can meet my stomach but the lifejacket is so tight and so rigid that I'm stuck sitting up straight. Michael tells me to focus on the horizon. I hear his voice but can't find his face. I'd closed my eyes. I open them, straighten further, think about what it means to be tough. To walk with sea legs. To make it.

The seasickness gets worse when I see the spikes of the islands dart up into the horizon. The boat is rising and falling with the ocean, making the islands grow huge and then disappear, magnify and slip away.

I know the Farallon Islands are mysterious, maybe haunted—unusual, striking, called the "Devil's Teeth." I know this is the type of place people whisper about and want to get close to. And when I see the islands for the first time it's as if my mind glitches and sees a picture, not a real part of the world. A memory, not the actual. Spikes rise out of the ocean. Rock pyramids, sand-colored and deep gray, coming out of the water like the ground being made. All lined up, some too circular, a row of oceanic planets. Birds squawk and swoop in circles around the islands' peaks. There's another sound too, a deep honking, as if a chorus of laughter was filtered through a French horn. A smell hits me, equal parts sulphur and salt water. It shoots up my nose, making it crinkle.

The approach puts a terrible feeling in me, a ringing of the internal bell of intuition, as Erin would say. Intuition is fine and easy to manage when I have the option to respond to its signals, but it's too late for that, there's no possible no now, so as the islands get bigger, the inside warning gets stronger, me angling directly toward the threat. Vomit is stuck in my throat; I refuse to let it out.

My legs buzz with adrenaline. The boat slowly comes to a stop and its momentum shifts backward into a float. Up ahead, what looked like a flat row of islands has tilted on a diagonal—the largest one, Southeast Farallon, sits in front, the even ground of it, where we are going, ten or twenty feet high. I can make out, behind it, to the left, another island of comparable size, separated by a skinny channel. Even Southeast Farallon, which I've heard Michael call SEFI, is surrounded by smaller rocks, tips and sharp edges careening over the flat top, as if the island is constantly splintering and making new bodies, islets that crowd the waters. No wonder the sailboat crashed. No wonder people aren't allowed here.

My ears tickle. Then the back of my neck. Flies crawl over my knees and into my hair. There are flies everywhere, on all surfaces, especially the human ones.

The waves crash hard against the sides of the rocks, sending mist over the flat part of the island. We wait. I see Michael's jeans and his boots in front of me. He's there to un-clip me. I don't know if I want this freedom again, but I shove the vomit down and nod and slowly stand. My legs are no longer legs. They're machines I don't know how to operate. I use them, for the moment, as props and stilts. I can stay standing. Michael squeezes my arm. I hear a loud whistle from the back, and I find my duffel bag and backpack and make my way to the stern, where two men, one a skinny guy with a mustache who doesn't seem much older than me, the other a man with a battered Nets hat and flannel over his fleece, work together to get the smaller boat into the water. Michael explains they use the smaller boat, a beat-up fishing boat with a white hard top, to tag and identify great white sharks by taking photos of their dorsal fins.

The gray rock is closer. The honking surrounds. That feeling is rising in me, loud and anxious.

I step into the tagging boat, where the water gets much, much closer. I fumble for a seated place. The boat can't be much longer than the sharks we're here to watch—twenty feet? The hard top covers the controls—a steering wheel, a digital navigation system, a radio—and some of the front in shade. There's a worn leather seat good for two butts, maybe, behind the wheel. Around the controls, there are thin lanes on each side, then benches that fold up to reveal storage compartments. Nets hat is shoving his bag into one of them. When he turns and sees me, he snickers and goes to take my bag, then stops himself—"May I?" "Yeah, please," I tell him, "Thank you," letting him take all my belongings and push them into a small space away from me, feeling stripped of most protection, wondering what it was about me or my face that made him laugh.

The boat's front is pointed but before that, flat and even—good for standing, balancing, watching, tagging. I picture myself out there, holding onto the silver railing, reaching for a huge animal swimming by.

As soon as everyone clamors aboard, the boat shifting as it adjusts to our weight, I meet the team. Nets hat is a tour guide for the islands who also dives for sea urchins. He used to be a professional harpoon fisherman. He's worked on Michael's expeditions sporadically over the years. A sometimes boat captain who has been face to face with a great white. Who thinks it's a warm day today. I shiver and hold my breath trying to contain it. "Will," he growls, "—is the name, but you can call me Captain."

Mustache is Zeke, a graduate student, this trip's research assistant. With a Free Palestine t-shirt and a bucket hat that ties at his chin. It's not his first time in the field. He looks at me a little bit like the guys at pickup basketball do. His polite smile gestures at respect but really equals tolerance. He's disappointed to be stuck guarding me. He's nice enough not to say it but not nice enough not to think it. I'm tall enough that he will try, because there's the tiny real fear that he could embarrass himself. Zeke stands up straighter, nodding at me and showing me the underside of his chin.

Michael is the head researcher here, our leader. "This is going to be fun," Michael says. "And educational. I promise." He clears his throat. "Now—and I mean this seriously—hold on." I grip the bench with one hand and the railing behind me with the other. "I'm Lydia," I tell them, before Captain takes the controls and pushes us forward in little bursts, timing it with the swells so that a big wave doesn't crash us into the rocks. As the tagging boat approaches the island, I see that the rock it's made of isn't as solid up close: there are holes everywhere, holes I can see the full round shape of, holes that seem to burrow so deep they lead all the way back underwater. Messy layers of moss, kelp, and other green organisms cover the rock's surface in patches, and when I look down, the water is interrupted at points by underwater cliffs, granite jutting out, covered in brightly colored everything: there are oranges, pinks, and reds, seaweed waving in all directions.

There is a loud mechanical sound and then above us, a crane—a huge metal hand attached to a bunch of ropes that swing out over the water and then our boat. The hand with its strings hovers over Captain, who grabs hold and starts attaching it to us with a series of massive yellow carabiners. The crane is how we get on and off the island. The coast is too rocky to safely dock anywhere and the waves would eat up a wooden dock if they ever tried to put one in. The bigger boat that brought us here is getting smaller in the distance; soon it will disappear.

I hold onto the ropes on the edges of the tagging boat as water flies in my face and the sky is reoriented over the ocean. I want to tell Zeke that I like his shirt—to establish that we're on the same team. But to have him as my teammate is something I earn, not what I say, so I stay quiet. The crane lifts us up, some faraway metal whining as it does. I am above the water now, above the surface, closer to the sky now than the land. I am in the in between. Gripping the ropes tightly, I peer over the side, where ten feet below us, a wave slams into the rocks. The spray reaches my face, my nose. Then the crane breaks ground—we are lifted above the island's flat surface, maneuvered over concrete. Zeke slaps a fly off his neck. Michael pulls another from the strands of his hair and flicks it into the air. There are flies all over Captain's hat and face—he does nothing.

"Welcome to East Landing," Captain bellows, scattering the closest few. "Wind's on our side today."

"Yeehaw," Michael says quietly. His belt buckle is a dirty gold, a tiny bull carved into the metal.

Captain expertly drops us onto a layer of rubber tires stacked on top of each other, a makeshift landing pad. The boat squeaks in. The water is very blue—and white, and gray, and sometimes green—while the island is mostly dust. Dirt and dust and rock. Some moss. Some muddy grass. Invasive weeds. Dead birds and clumps of feathers and bird shit. It is not a place for people. It's loud—birds squawking, seals honking, waves slamming and fizzing, flies buzzing into my ear canal, wind whistling, so loud that I find myself reading lips, as if there's almost no room for our sounds.

Before we step off the boat, Michael hands out brushes and bleach wipes. "For your shoes," he says, "To make sure nothing on the mainland hitched a ride."

We grab our bags and follow a slight trail into a barren valley. This flat stretch of land, the size of a couple football fields, is traversable via concrete path—three feet across, the concrete crumbling and eroding—that cuts neatly through the grass and dirt and rock, making a very minimal grid. I trace the path across to where it gives way into dirt, a line that weaves in zigzags up a very steep hill to an old lighthouse. At some points there's a railing, wooden and splintery. The hill looks too steep to take straight on. The lighthouse leers over us, the hill hundreds of feet high, the sides shaky with loose rock. There are barely any signs here, only the ones warning that this is a protected area.

We step onto the concrete path and follow it straight and then to the right—in the middle of that flat stretch, beyond which waves are visible, more rocks, and more water, there are two houses that look like ghosts. They are big and square with chimneys poking up from each, flanked on their sides by lone trees, slightly sad and wilting. They're the only trees I can see on island.

Captain leads. My hair whips around my chin and spirals around my ears. Strands get stuck in my mouth. I hold onto the straps of my backpack and follow. Captain laughs at me again. "Smells bad huh?"

"What?"

"You're holding your breath."

"Oh. Fuck, I—"

"One of the largest colonies of seabirds in North America nests on these islands. Think of all that bird shit. Hell yeah, it smells."

Michael keeps his gaze down as he walks, his fingers looped into his jeans, the back pockets faded and worn. I examine him again, seeing that older version of Julian, one who knows more, has lived more, who has more to offer. This one has broader shoulders, a deeper voice, softer jeans, and kinder eyes.

When I step onto the island and smell the bird shit, when I hike across the rocky land to find the two houses, twin horror movies in an empty field, when I get into the shared room I will be staying in and the sound of the wind continues as if there are no walls or windows, the room in which I will be sleeping the next twelve weeks, I realize it's not a joke anymore, or even an obsession; there I am in my body, a surprise.

Inside, all the windows are closed, but there is somehow still a draft. It's our first night here and I'm nervous. Nervous about sharing a room with my new co-worker, nervous about sleeping at all with the sounds of the wind, nervous about waking up on time tomorrow morning and doing a good enough job. I'm sharing a house with these men, these men that I don't know, save for Michael, and right now, shivering into my sweatshirt, the idea seems crazy and entirely right—for these problems to be mine, not others, for this place to be where I live and work.

Before I left, my best friend Tasia wrote me a postcard that I still haven't read. I tape the postcard up next to our window. The bed is bunked, shoved tight against the wall in a room I share with Zeke. The sun is setting now, making everything around us orange, enveloping us in rust. The horizon is a clear bright line under the sun, a long rectangle of preserved air. Our window directly faces the other house, more battered than our own, no longer habitable.

I brush my teeth, scrub my face with witch hazel and brush my hair. I pull my beanie over my ears as I climb up and into bed. The ceiling is close. I try to touch it with the tip of my nose. I can't manage that, but I do graze my forehead. The skin on my neck stretches and there's a click in back. My body falls into the bed. The wood shakes and creaks. Zeke picked the bottom bunk, and I didn't protest. I can hear him breathing down there, and I try to get my body to stop: breathing, moving, giving proof I'm up here.

There's no cell service but there's Wi-Fi, strong enough to text and check email. Michael has asked us to limit our personal use to at night when all the work is done. We'll each get to make a weekly call from a satellite phone. I told Erin I'd use it to call her. She doesn't know we have internet access. I don't know if Tasia expects me to call—she's probably busy, anyway, with her new sorority at UCSB. When she came to the funeral, a few weeks into the school year, her skin was tan and clear and her teeth seemed whiter than usual, and I couldn't help but think about how happy she was with all the new girls in her life. I know she loved Blake, and it's not that she wasn't sad, but she couldn't leave her new happiness behind either; it glowed from the inside and I resented her for it. After everyone was gone, I huddled with her in the Buddhist temple parking lot and picked my cuticles bloody until she slapped my hand away. I told her I was coming here and she looked at me like she didn't recognize me. For years she had been telling me to get bangs, that my face shape could pull it off.

I check my phone. I could send a text—describe my room to Tasia, tell Erin I got here. I hold down the side buttons until it turns off.

The waves are so loud it's as if they're breaking over the house. It's close enough that it feels like separating a cause from its effect— I'm stepping into water but my legs aren't wet. My eyes are closed, waiting for the spray to fall on top of me in this creaky bed, soaking through the quilt, the two layers of blankets, my extra pair of socks. I pull the quilt over my beanie and retell myself the story of the outside of this house. That it was re-built and made stronger.

My moms completely rebuilt the house I grew up in. Blake was a carpenter before she learned to code and changed careers. The house was halfway up Marin Ave., a street so steep it felt like riding a rollercoaster on the way down. The backyard was one big slope, where the house gave way to hillside. Dusty, no grass, quick to fill up with eucalyptus leaves. In scattered boxes throughout our base-ment, there are old film prints of the houses Blake worked on, spaces caught in different stages of a process, but I could never differentiate the before from the after.

The light bleeds through the window shade in the early morning, through the walls, the house a lantern.

Downstairs, Zeke retrieves two slices of toast from the toaster and rubs butter onto them. He asks me: "You're still in high school?"

I tell him I graduated a few months ago.

"How'd you get this job?"

I don't know how to respond.

"I mean, how'd you find out about this job?"

"I know his son," I say, lying less. "I'm going to Berkeley." Here I am closer to a college student than a high schooler, and I know Michael more than I knew Julian. Zeke gives me a weird look.

"I deferred," I explain. My chest tightens.

Most of the rooms in this house are off—mis-matched furniture fills the living room, the workroom hosts computers so old it's like a period piece in there. I heard mice squeaking in the corners of our room last night. The kitchen, though, is beautiful. Spacious and open, with a long countertop, the walls full of hanging pans and pots and colorful potholders.

I haven't done anything like this before—Michael knows that. So does Zeke, apparently, even though he hasn't been told. I don't quite know what my role is as intern, except that I'm here to be another set of hands and eyes, someone who makes hard things easier. Maybe that's why I jump to making breakfast. In his rundown, Michael talked about cooking but didn't specify who would do it. He said this team is a unique one because it's so small with so much to do. If you can do anything, don't hesitate. Do it. And so I do it, except I do the simplest version of breakfast because I don't want to have to clean up too much, and I don't want to be judged for my cooking either.

I boil eggs for me, Captain, and Michael, and when I'm done, I wash the pot and rinse off the sink. Cleaning supplies are sparse. I get the sense we're supposed to be neat but that everything is going to stay kind of dirty.

At home, I was responsible for scrubbing the mold off the tiles in the shower once a month. I'd put on thick rubber gloves and use bleach, not the natural stuff. After it was done, Blake would float into my room and tell me, "It smells good in the bathroom." Excessive cleanliness might be slowly killing us, all that staring into bleach as we scrub. All those deep breaths to get more of a good smell, which is really no smell. We want to smell that everything is missing: dirt, grime, shit. We want to smell the destruction of something, or maybe to smell nothing at all. I imagine myself in our clean bathroom, where I sit in the absence of smell, alone. I wait for the door to open, for Blake to enter without knocking, but there is nothing.

Michael bites into his hard-boiled egg, wipes yolk off the sides of his mouth, and claims that he loves the smell here. The yolk was runny on his skin. Did I undercook the eggs? He squints out the kitchen window. He pushes his hair away from his face, and steam rises from his coffee. The skin of his hands is red where it bends to squeeze the handle. I like those hands.

"How are you feeling this morning?" He asks me, voice booming. "Getting used to island time?"

"I'm feeling great," I tell him, smiling with my lips closed, tightening the muscles in my jaw. I'm game to be someone here who I'm not at home—ready, amenable, future-forward, with a positive attitude. I stand up straighter and maintain direct eye contact, feeling in me how willing I am to change myself for Michael. It's dumb because lesbians, lesbian moms in particular, are the most can-do—I was raised inside that imagination.

"I don't know if I like the smell, but I like the way the air feels," I tell him. Michael nods in agreement, then salutes me with his coffee cup, satisfied.

"You'll get used to it."

Captain walks me from the kitchen, past the thrift store living room and the computer museum into the small back room, where he shows me the second fridge and freezer. I flip through the categories of frozen food—old plastic-wrapped chicken, frost-burned slices of bread, crumpled frozen pizzas. There's fish, too. A lot of it. Contained frozen bodies lying on their sides, encased in plastic. The fish is probably for bait, but for baiting what I'm not sure.

"Is that for the sharks?"

"No, you can't chum here."

"What's chum?"

"Blood, fish parts, bone—a mix that gets the sharks out. Cage divers used to use it, but they're not allowed anymore. Doesn't stop everybody though."

"Gotcha."

My fingertips go numb, and I remove my hands from the freezer. My nails are painted. My hands are too nice.

Stacked in the living room is the tagging gear—sticks connected to underwater cameras, a seal decoy made out of thick plastic and gray-brown carpeting. A shark falls for that? It looks like a rug dreamed up a sea creature. Captain sees the question in my head.

"Works every time," he says.

Harpoon is a word that exists as more myth than object in my head. Harpoon lives in the hands of a fisherman killing a whale in the center of a brutal storm, water flying, large beard obscuring his grimace. Lightning strikes the water. Whale goes down. Blood and fat spray from the wound.

But here is a harpoon, a shining aluminum pole, resting against the floor of the house where I now live. The aluminum pole brassy at its front end. I worry about the floor getting scratched. Captain reaches for it with rough and deliberate hands. I ask what I can carry. He tells me the camera gear and the decoy. Then, with both hands clasped around the harpoon, its body resting against his chest, the sharp end tilting over his shoulder, he asks me if I want to learn. I adjust myself and crack my chest across the sternum.

"Yes. Does it hurt?"

"Who?"

"The shark."

Captain curls and uncurls his right pinky, shaking his head. "No ma'am. We tag sharks the right way." His pinky is crooked, veering off to the right. The middle joint is swollen. He explains to me that the tags we'll use are called satellite archival pop-up tags, short-term tags that stick to the animal for a limited period and then release, sending data back to us once it hits the water's surface.

"You wanna be a scientist or what?"

"Maybe."

His head twists and shifts down into a hearty nod, smiling like I've given him a gift. He shakes out his pinky, wincing, then curls it back up.

"Well, you can't tag any sharks yourself, but I can show you what goes into it. It's mostly about timing. And precision. I'm a good shot. Obviously, we don't use the normal lily, it's one of Michael's needles that we load up with a tag. Goes right into the base of thedorsal fin." Captain points to a spot on his own body, the bony, rounded top of his neck.

I nod. My hand reaches up to my own neck. It says something about Captain that he's telegraphing the shark's body onto his, even as he's targeting them with an object that hurts. I don't believe it doesn't hurt.

Outside, the sunlight floods the fog. It's as if we are hidden under a blanket. I have a plastic case of gear in my arms, I have my rainjacket on. I have my hair tied back under my bandana so nothing flies around my face. There's the smell again, stronger. There's the loud squawking of birds. The roof has a thick layer of bird shit over it, an extra shield. I hike up the case and use my hip as a shelf to get a good grip. I try to control my face, but Zeke sees it and laughs. He says, not meanly, "You'll get it." Then the case slips a half inch and his face changes. "You need a hand?" It's not the type of offer you accept.

We march back to the crane, where our boat will be lowered into the water. It's still foggy. The wind is cold. The spray of ocean water is cold. I tell myself, "You're not cold."

The purpose of our research is to learn more about great white sharks—to know more is to better protect the sharks, I'm told. We are adding to and keeping up with the catalog of great whites off the California coast. Counting, recognizing, and using our imagination. Our days will go like this: wake up, eat, clean up, suit up (layer up), crane out, try to tag, take photos, identify sharks, eat on boat, crane back, organize data, eat at house, clean up, sleep. Fall and winter is shark season here. There can be multiple shark attacks a week, in which case we'll boat out to the site and write a record of what we see.

If we've got extra hands at the end of the day, we'll send one man to higher ground, where they'll scan the waters with a radio, looking to report attacks. Otherwise, we rely on the larger ecosystem of Michael's friends—boats passing through and around the islands, captained by men who might throw Michael a bone and radio in a sighting. Most of the sharks, Michael says, we'll already know. The same sharks have been coming here for years. We're watching for distinctive markings on the fins.

Michael and Captain hook the crane to the tagging boat and it lowers us into the water. Captain turns over the motor and we zip across the surface. Mist hits my face. I zip my rain jacket higher. Across from me, Zeke wears work boots that go halfway up his calves. His head is tilted to the side, looking where we're headed, his gaze steady and straight. His face is tan and slim with cheekbones that cut into his cheeks, gaunt and serious. I feel slippery against the hard edges of the boat and the movement of the water; the bumps, when we hit them, are like bouncing against concrete.

The island shrinks slightly as we pull away. Birds circle overhead. The sound is, again, overwhelming—like a crowd yelling at you. Part of me thought remote meant quiet, space meant alone. We sleep in bunk beds and the sound never goes away.

Captain narrates as he drives, "We're passing Jewel Cave, on our left, home to one of many tidepools on the islands." Through the mist, the land separates, and down a narrow passage, slopes to where it meets the ocean in a foamy mess. I can't see any tidepools, only murky seawater. Zeke cocks his head at me and tells me, "They're underwater right now. Called an intertidal zone."

"Got it." I hope I'm not the girl who knows nothing, leaving myself open to boys who claim they're teachers.

"And onto Shubrick Point..." As Captain speaks, the landscape rounds into a massive hill, and soon the old lighthouse is looming over us, its concrete speckled with algae. I feel very small and suddenly anxious. When we round Shubrick Point, putting the lighthouse slightly behind us, Captain cuts the motor, which makes a half-hearted buzzing noise as it fades. The boat stops, and the waves pick us up, rocking us gently back and forth as we slow to a float. Michael motions to me. I move away from Zeke and over to him at the front. To move around the boat, we move around each other, brushing limbs, equipment, boots.

"Let me walk you through this," Michael says, "It's all timing." He pulls the seal decoy out, attaches an underwater camera to the bottom layer, fixes the decoy to a line, and throws the line a few feet from the boat. The fake seal hits the water flatly, right-side up. It wiggles in the water, moving like a Jell-O version of the real thing. The water is shallow around the islands—at some points, so shallow you can see the bottom of the ocean from the boat.

Captain starts up the engine and Michael lets the line go slack as Captain pulls us ten feet out, then stops. The line clicks and clicks and clicks, then goes quiet. Ten feet doesn't seem far enough. Then Michael turns to me and hands me the pole. "What's different about this kind of decoy from, say, a rubber one like they use in South Africa, is that we don't actually want the sharks to bite it. Think of it as a lure. We want to see the sharks as clearly as possible for as long as possible, and then save the camera."

The metal and plastic tucks into the corner of my elbow, the side of my hip. I need good grip, I need to be ready. "Okay," I say, "Okay."

"Do you have any questions?"

"When do you know it's time to save the camera? To pull it in?"

"Sharks are even faster than you think. Captain will signal you and then you give it all you got to bring that line in. You're strong." He nudges my shoulder, teasing me. "Time to put those basketball muscles to work."

I nod, "Okay. I got it." I wish I had more questions to ask—I want him to keep talking—but it's pretty simple, my next task. Bring the line the fuck in, as fast as I can, before a shark swallows our fake seal.

A shape comes into our water, dark and rounded, moving quickly. My chest stutters. I hold tight to the decoy line. Then the shape slows, and a head emerges through the foam: a sea lion, its face curious, with round black eyes and long whiskers. It disappears under the water again, swimming up to the decoy, poking at it with its nose, and moving on toward the boat. I look over the edge and there it is swimming next to us, breaking the surface. It makes a full circle around us before it leaves. The water foams up and the boat tilts. My feet and knees try to adjust to the movement of the water, of creatures in the water. On the boat there is the constant re-finding of balance.

I can sense myself smiling. I feel stupid and try to make my face neutral again.

For a while it's quiet. Captain whistles, a sweet, rounded sound that comes out of his mouth fully formed. Michael scans our surroundings, as does Zeke. I try to follow suit, but I'm so attached to my line and pole that adrenaline has made us the same machine. I hold better than I keep watch.

Then everyone on the boat is moving. Michael has yelled, "Got one!" Zeke has binoculars pressed to his face. Captain's gaze is relaxed but fixed in front of us. About twenty feet past the decoy is a fin, huge and foreboding, connected to a large body, its sides rounded and massive, gray-black rubber through the water. In the same moment I see the shark, I immediately imagine it sees me.

I learned I was claustrophobic in the fourth grade when Tasia crawled into the large pipe on the edge of our elementary school playground and I followed. The pipe was hidden by green tangles of weeds and spiderwebs and we thought it connected to the high school we shared a fence with. Tasia, who's always been small and slim, crawled in first, surprising both of us, and I followed, immediately ripping the knees of my jeans and the first layer of skin underneath. The pipe smelled like rust, or blood, sourer even than that, and it was so small my head hit the top if I propped myself onto my elbows.

Tasia went quickly, army-crawling until I could barely make out the grooves of her sneakers. The pipe was dark and I got stuck. I don't know if my foot got caught, or my muscles decided to shut down on account of fear, but I was genuinely, truly stuck—dread filling my body as if bloating it with water. I imagined myself growing and swelling, my bones multiplying inside me until I occupied every open space of that pipe, and the fear and dread spread like clay in my throat.

When the first shark comes, I am back in that tunnel, my throat full of clay, my body fear. Intuition ringing loud inside me. The fin breaks the surface and I'm still standing there. The fin has broken the surface and my body will not move. The fin weaves fast toward the decoy and there is no one to tug me out of the boat by my shoes. The decoy is attached to the line and the line is in my hands and the bones inside me are swelling. If the shark makes it to the fake seal and bites, I will feel it. There is nowhere to go.

Captain yells, "Reel it in!"

Everything leaks out—the clay, the bones, the fear—and I just go. The line clicks as I whirl the lever around, pulling the decoy across the water and closer to us. Michael makes a signal to Captain, then strides to the other end of the boat to get a better angle on the shark, where he smiles, yelling back to Captain, voice hoarse with sudden happiness, "See that scar?"

"That who I think it is?"

As the shark moves, something violent in the way the water's barely disturbed, a slicing, Captain grips the harpoon. The shark is close to us: huge, nearly the length of our boat. The way it moves reminds me of a snake, its power and force contained in the sides, everything wiggling, faster than seems possible. I get the decoy up the edge of the boat and then inside. The force and momentum knock me on my ass. It doesn't matter, though—I saved the camera.

Meanwhile Michael is on the left side of the boat, the long tripod extended into the water like an oar. And Captain—well, he leans his body over the other side, reaches over, and jabs the harpoon. When Captain pulls the pole back and his upper half is again visible to me, the tag is gone. "Told you I was a good shot."

I pick myself up and slide into a seat next to Zeke. Zeke fills in a data sheet, a neat graph on a slightly shiny piece of paper. The time, a description of the shark, its name, our location (in between rocks? Shubrick Point? Where the water is a slightly darker blue?), estimated water temperature, salinity, and depth, as well as the number of the successful tag. He retrieves these wild pieces of data incredibly fast. Then he turns to me. His t-shirt is orange under his layers. The color reflects onto the underside of his chin and ears. "You ready?" I don't move fast enough and he quickly speaks to fill the space. "The decoy."

I scramble up, hoisting the pole up my body, shaking the decoy out and making sure it's attached properly, striding to the front. Zeke watches me closely from the back of the boat and this time he charitably says, "Good, good," then, editing himself, "Good enough. You know, you could adjust your grip—" Captain, hearing this, barks at him: "She's got it." Michael pulls the tripod camera back into the boat with gloved hands and I cast the decoy out.

The decoy floats and we wait for the next shark. Michael's hand nearly comes down to my shoulder. Even though we face the same ocean, he will spot the next shark before I do. The wind rustles his hair. His skin is freckled underneath the sunburn. Warmth spreads in my stomach. Michael takes a deep breath. His chest goes up and down. He floats his arms over his head and lets them fall to his sides. His irises are dark, the eyelashes long. The bottom of a well. The end of a tunnel. The ground.

Michael warns us to stay vigilant. Sharks hang around the islands all year, but the population explodes in the fall. We are in the middle of the shark rush, when the most sharks come to the islands. It will seem unthinkable, the number of sharks that we'll see.

"That was Bite Size, right?" Zeke says.

Michael nods. "That guy's consistent. We see him just about every year."

"Why Bite Size?" I ask.

Captain traces a half circle around his left eye with his finger. Michael says, "He's got a healed bite mark around his face, from another white shark. Probably a sister."

"Like a family fight?"

The men laugh. "You'll get used to the shark lingo. A sister is—"

"A woman shark, a big girl," Captain fills in. "Female sharks tend to be bigger than males."

"And they think," Zeke says, excited, "That white sharks might bite each other when they mate."

Ignoring Zeke, I ask, "Why are the female sharks bigger?"

Michael answers, "They need the extra size to carry their young. White sharks give birth to live young—born at five or so feet long."

"Are white sharks a kind of great white? Like mini ones? I didn't know there were multiple types."

Zeke laughs and returns to his sheet, Captain to the controls, moving past me, leaving Michael and me up front. Michael explains that the scientific community dropped the "great," making the new common name just, "white shark." "Better for shark PR," he jokes. "Less scary."

I make myself small against the bench seats, then tug at Michael's sleeve and ask him, quietly, imagining that I can engineer a moment of privacy on this boat, "Wait. What if the great white— white shark—ate the decoy? Would it die? Choke?"

Michael shakes his head sadly. "Sharks' stomachs are full of plastic nowadays. Plus, they might take a bite and not swallow it. We used to use foam surf boards—you should've seen the carnage."

I nod, how naïve of me, to think one decoy rug could push a shark over the edge. Michael continues, "We aren't in the business of feeding sharks plastic. It's just to get them close enough to us."

Michael pulls out a slim leather journal and a pencil, to document Bite Size and his approach, I'm guessing, but I'd like to keep talking, and I ask him if he ever sees full shark families out here. It's clear that he's ready to start his notes, but this question gets him excited, "No, no, white sharks aren't social in that way. They're primarily loners—though sometimes you'll see two sharks swimming together for a while, and there hasn't been enough research done on whether that proximity is just that—proximity—or there's real learning and communication happening. Plus," he says, "Juvenile sharks like warm water. This is too cold for them."

"Do they learn anything from their parents?"

"No. They have to fend for themselves from the very moment they're born."

Michael stops then, gives me an apologetic look, and sits down to get to his notes. His journal is a deep brown, scratched up with its own scars. Taped on the bottom corner is a phrase in Sharpie: "#1 OF 5." Will he fill five journals when he's here? Are the other four for different parts of our work here? I lean against the railing and watch the decoy, wondering how a baby shark knows what to do— if it feels its body as a surprise.

Fathers, I haven't seen them do much. I didn't grow up in a house with one. When I visited friends who had fathers, like Tasia and her dad Eugene, they asked dumb questions and then went to sit in the living room with a book. They were bad at handy stuff, hopeless compared to Blake at fixing a sink. It seemed the job description was: "Hang around. Try to help and do it badly. Then don't worry about it. Remember to smile." They seemed sort of extra, super-fluous, floating. They got to fuck up more and it was funny when they did it. Eugene was older, too, nearly seventy by the time we graduated, so maybe he was a bad example—too tired to do much of anything at all.

What makes a failure is feeding sharks a meal of plastic, of losing the reason that sharks would choose to be near us in the first place. Every day we get into the water and ask sharks to get close, and then closer.

At the end of the day we've tagged one more shark and identified another. The shark names could be better, honestly. Someone called the shark with a spot under his eye Boxer but he could have been Cry Baby.

For all the adrenaline of the first approach, the day was long and slow. With empty time. Sometimes I found my chin tipping upward and then I was staring at the sky. Watching the fog move, searching for blue or the fuzzy orb of white light that is the sun behind clouds. Michael says: "It's normal, it's normal, it's normal." And: "Ninety-nine percent of this job is waiting."

Back at the house, we eat dinner downstairs all together. Our hands are wet and wrinkled. The wind is loud outside. The water tastes weird—researchers gather it themselves all winter. I wonder what Blake would say about that, if I told her we drank gathered water. She might make a face, scrunch her nose up. Erin will be interested in how it's purified, in what has to be brought to the island and what's available here.

We made chili. To go with it we are eating box-mix cornbread and drinking cans of Coke. When I lift the Coke to my lips it tastes like salt water. When I eat the cornbread with my hands, it tastes like bird shit. Zeke tells me I can try to soak my fingernails to get them clean, that it helps with the smell.

Captain makes Michael laugh and he opens his mouth before realizing there is still food in it—but he's laughing so hard that he can't keep it closed, so there's this ridiculous cycle of open mouth to closed mouth to a bobbing of the head, nearly obsessive, to swallow, and repeat. Is he going to spit out his food all over the table? The inside of his mouth is red. One of his back teeth is silver. His forehead is sunburnt pink, and sweaty, the edges by his hairline starting to peel.

Zeke doesn't laugh as easily—he's serious and he keeps his face in the same expression most of the time. He's a third year PhD student at Berkeley, studying marine biology. He graduated college and went right to grad school, with no time in between. I bet this is the kind of work he wants to do forever. He sips his water and leans slightly back in his chair. He asks Captain if he's reached any new breath holding records. Captain says no. His best is still eight minutes. Eight minutes underwater!

"Yeah," he says, "You have to learn how to breathe first."

"I know how to breathe," I say.

"Not like this," he says.

I shake my head and chug more of my soda. My body is tired. I keep hearing the same acronym thrown around in grumpy tones of voice—MARO. MARO is the nonprofit with the most access to these islands, the group that, in collaboration with US Fish & Wildlife, made and makes Michael's research here possible. Michael's research runs on "soft money"—money that comes from grant to grant instead of a salary at a university.

"I was trained as an ornithologist," Michael says, "I get it. I was a bird guy first."

"Really?" Zeke didn't know that.

"Yeah. I was a very green bird researcher, and a friend of mine was doing a survey of the birds on West End Island." That's the second island I saw when we got here, separated via channel from ours. "If you think our part of the island is rugged, wait until you see West End. There's nothing but birds. Huge amounts of fur seals too, who don't come on this island, maybe because they don't like people too much."

Captain cracks his neck and adjusts his seat, listening. Zeke fidgets, eager to jump in but forcing patience. Michael tells us how he spent a summer careful not to step on bird nests and even birds themselves, burrowed into the rock just deep enough you think it's safe to step. Every night, they'd return to SEFI, where they'd pile into the house, make an easy dinner, and pass out.

"And sometimes, on our return, I'd pass the other research team—the other house was being used at that time, maintained properly—and say a few words. Just a couple pleasantries, a five-minutes-a-day kind of relationship."

"What were they there to do?" I ask.

"Elephant seal tagging."

I want to gloat, as this is the part of the story that tips Michael into history I already know. I nod, knowingly, holding this familiarity close.

"There was a woman who ran the elephant seal team, and they were short-staffed. The more and more I'm there, the more I find I'm waiting until those five minutes to find out what she did that day. I'm dreaming about the other side of the channel, right?" He takes a sip of water, then continues. "Finally, one day, she asks me—they need an extra set of hands, can I help out? Just for a day or two. I tell my friend, and my friend allows it, our boss somehow lets me go, and the creatures are bigger, over there, the animals are unrulier, and I'm even more exhausted at the end of the day."

"Were you sleeping in the other house by the end of it too?" Captain asks, wry.

Michael looks at me, and then Zeke, considering it, then answers: "Yes. I want to say no, but yes, I was—I fell in love."

"Is that how you met your wife, er, ex-wife?" I ask, trying to put the pieces of Michael's life together in my head. This woman, the elephant seal tagger, wasn't in his first story, or maybe I erased her, if she was.

"No, it's not. The relationship didn't last long on land, or, out of research, rather. I think I loved her for what she showed me, what she brought me into—that was a massive act of love. No one had ever been so generous to me, in my entire life." Love, to Michael, meant being gifted a world. Tugged by hands into the deep end.

"I lost my point," Michael laments. "No, no, I had one—I can understand MARO's insistence on birds being the priority species here." Zeke and Captain groan in unison. "I can! Listen, we're lucky to be here. The elephant seals and sea lions have rookeries here, on the rocks, on the beaches, and the birds nest on the islands. The sharks don't. They just pass through. We still get funding every year—"

"Look at our team, man," Captain grumbles. "Is that really proper funding?"

"No, it's not," Michael admits. Around the table, Zeke sits with his legs crossed. His t-shirt has a hole in it around the neck. Captain slouches forward so his arms, hinged at the elbows, frame his plate. A winning team. "I have my existential worries too. It's just, I can understand it. I hope they keep seeing the bigger picture." Captain and Zeke murmur words of agreement. I didn't know our team was smaller than it was supposed to be—maybe in my replacing Julian, I must be both him and me, the force of two sets of hands, not one.

Captain asks Michael what he thinks his son is up to at home. His son—I feel a spike of joy in my chest. In this world he is a boy and a son. In my mind he shrinks. Michael tells us he'll be with his mom for the holidays. I knew Julian's parents were divorced, but he didn't really talk about it. I never met his mom.

"Have you spoken with him yet?" Michael asks. The bubble of the island quickly pops.

My face goes blank and red. "No," I say. "I haven't tried to use the satellite phone yet."

"It's easy," Michael says. "He'll show you," he says, meaning Zeke, who I can feel watching me curiously. Zeke nods.

"Thank you," I say, looking into my lap. "I really want to get settled first."

I raise my can as a half-toast and there is an extra question in Michael's expression. There's something here, a thick air that rushes into the space between us. Maybe he's wondering if Julian and I are fighting. Maybe it's not that. I hold his gaze and he pushes his can up as if toasting back.

I put my bowl into the sink, along with the other dishes I've cleared—grease slicks the inside of each bowl, sticky crumbs of corn-bread gathering at the edges. I cooked and I can leave these dishes, I can walk away right now, but then they won't be done, not at least until another person decides to do them, and the discomfort grows in my chest, the men still at the table, laughing now at some joke some-body told, the wind loud, me standing there.

I wash the dishes and then we all retreat to our rooms. There's no mirror in ours. The only access I have into how I look is the reflection of my body in the windows, which seems to make the edges double. When I pull my work pants off, I find there are oval bruises along the V where my hip bone meets muscle and stomach fat, where I pressed the pole to my right side, where I banged it against myself as I tugged the line in. Nothing hurt in the moment, but I wince as I push fingers into the blue circles now. I move quickly and the bruises disappear under a clean layer of clothing. I try not to get naked in here. If I have to undress, I'm smooshing my arms tight against my body and keeping everything private. It's like Zeke and I are sharing a corridor, a slim hallway that leads nowhere.

When Zeke's in the bathroom, I look into my window shape and try to give it permission. There is a chance I'm not myself on this island; there's also a chance this time here is the only opportunity I'll get to see who or what I actually am, without a history that is long and tedious and obscuring, a ribbon of intention and ex-pectation around everything I do. Tasia knew me better than anyone, which means she thinks she can predict what I want and need. I'm conditioned to replicate the version of myself that she loves, which is to say the me that she knows. What if I intend to be different? What if, in action, I am different, and she misses it, explains it away?

I'm in bed when Zeke asks me, "Lydia, are you dating Michael's son?" I hold my breath until I answer, telling him, "I mean, I was. We broke up." Silence from the lower bunk.

Julian didn't so much break up with me as let me leave. He chainsmoked cigarettes with asthma all summer and got pneumonia. The bacteria that gave him the pneumonia produced toxins that damaged his blood vessels and the vessels began to leak—his body went into septic shock. I didn't want to stay with him while he recovered. There was a small chance he'd need to have a procedure called thoracentesis, where a doctor sticks a needle right into the lungs and drains fluid from them, but it didn't seem likely. He just got a shit ton of antibiotics. If staying had meant being part of an actionable recovery, maybe I would have—I was interested in seeing the gunk literally pulled from his body—but what he asked for was my presence, for me to slip close to his clammy body and wait. I couldn't do that and he didn't understand.

"Does he know that?" Zeke asks.

"Julian? He broke up with me. So yes, he knows."

"No, I mean Michael."

"Of course he does."

A weird laugh escapes my mouth, my face hot in the dark. Zeke is quiet.

When I left for the boat in Julian's spot, even borrowing some of his gear, we didn't say we were broken up. We didn't say much of anything at all. I had the suspicion Julian was talking to his ex-girlfriend again, but I wasn't able to confirm it, so I walked away knowing the agreement between us was now tenuous, shaky, sticky, and if we wanted to pick it back up again, it wouldn't be totally crazy, but if everything had fundamentally changed between the two of us because of this choice, that wouldn't be either.

I check my email and there are the scraps of my old life—a late condolences note from a cousin on Erin's side, an email from the dean of students at Berkeley explaining what deferral will mean for registration two quarters from now, promotions from Staples, Nike, Urban Outfitters, Ross, and Sephora, a Google alert for Julian's name, which always pulls articles about the same not-Julian who's the president of the Astronomical Society of Greenbelt, Maryland, nothing from Tasia—and I shut my phone off again. It's too heavy in my hand. It's kind of clumsy. What a stupid piece of metal. I slide the phone against the wall until I hit the mattress and shove it underneath, pinching my fingers against the metal frame in the process.

"What was that?"

"Nothing."

The birds are yelling when I wake up in the morning. I scrub my face, brush my teeth, smell fish, plod downstairs, boil eggs and make coffee. Zeke makes toast again. He tells me he can tell what birds are making which yells. I wait for a sound I can pull out of the crowd. "That one. What's that bird?"

Zeke says: "Brandt's cormorant." I make sure not to stay in this closeness for too long, or he will start to realize that we're becoming friends.

The fog surrounds us as we walk with our supplies to the crane, to the boat, to the ocean. My hands move a little faster today: pull, attach, throw out, reel in, repeat. Make sure the camera didn't get too knocked around. The water is rockier. Our boat moves in sudden jolts, scaring the sea lions that approach us before the sharks come. My stomach turns along with the sea, along with the boat. My gut wants to choose a direction but the water doesn't comply. The ocean is not calm but balanced, and we aren't part of the balance. It doesn't think about us.

The hours pass slower when we're fucking up. Maybe Michael can sense that fuckup energy because when I nearly slice my finger on the line, moving too fast, he asks, "What's the majority of this job?" His face serious. Everything in me freezes. Reeling in a fake seal? Bracing for impact? My thoughts race. I don't want to be wrong, not to him. I know what he'd like me to say, "Waiting."

"You can slow down," he says, the seriousness breaking, and there's room for me again. "You're doing great."

Michael decrees that we break for lunch. I un-zip my backpack and pull out the salad I packed in a dumb little Tupperware container. The metal fork is stuck in a crevice of my pack but I dig for it until I get it and wipe it off on the decoy-wet parts of my pants. I crack open the Tupperware. It's sad. The greens are wilted to the sides. We won't have fresh produce for long—it'll run out before our next supplies delivery. With the container between my thighs, I jab at pieces of lettuce and try to bring them to my mouth—you know, eat.

I fail. The boat rocks, the greens drop. The boat jolts, my fork goes into my face and not my mouth.

Zeke busts out laughing. It's a loud sound that echoes, friendly and elastic like a duck. His shoulders shake and tears quickly go to his eyes.

"What?"

Zeke laughs so hard he can't speak. He just shakes his head at me, exhaling in long chunks. Captain tells me, "General rule is to not bring anything you can't eat with your hands."

"Fork—" Zeke tries to say. "Fork's not your friend."

Then the water pushes the boat again and I lose my fork in between slats of wood that seem sure to splinter. When I reach into the wooden bottom of boat and stretch my fingers for the feeling of fork-metal, not wanting to find face Zeke, Captain, and Michael, I start to laugh. Then we are all laughing and I abandon my utensil. The sound is enveloping, each one of us a part. Michael seems to find me in the middle of it all, his gaze kind. My eyes water.

One of our voices drops out and the collective laugh is over. Captain says in a low voice: "We've got one."

But the decoy's not even out. What does the shark want? We get to our feet, fan out across the boat. I have nothing to do without my decoy so Zeke tugs the sleeve of my rain jacket and tells me I can take field notes with him. I find my backpack, unzip it, racing to find my notebook. In the event of a shark attack, I am rushing to find a pad of paper; it feels absurd, but it's something to do, what I've been told to do, a way to be useful. When I find the notebook, I hustle to the bench seats with Zeke.

My chest has not yet gotten used to this new proximity to sharks. This shark doesn't move like a freight train but glides, a shadow beneath the surface, its fin pushing slightly upwards. This shark looks smaller than the ones we saw yesterday. When the fin breaks the water, I can see it has a strange shape, the back edge has a neat half-circle missing.

The fin disappears, the shark hanging as if suspended just below the choppy top of the water. It swims slowly up to us, its size threatening that of our boat, even though this shark is much smaller than others we've seen. This animal is much slower, more curious, gentle, its approach detached from the forward death drive of Bite Size, all energy funneling into the decoy.

The boat shifts in the water. Captain makes a booming sound as he readies the harpoon, leans over the edge of the boat, his stomach softening over the railing, and jabs it. The shark seems to shudder and dart away, but then returns just as quickly, gliding in parallel to us and the waves for what registers as a long time.

"I want to get a closer look," I tell Zeke, who I can see is writing a list of distinct details: notches on fin, scarring on flanks, heavier on left, small chunk of fin missing, malnourished? His handwriting is neat and all-caps, using every available bit of the page. He barely registers me. "Okay." Then, after the slightest pause, "You know you retain information better when you write it down." He glances up. This asshole. Michael could see Zeke admonishing me and agree or get the idea that I'm fucking around. I drop my voice low and tell him, "Obviously. I need to see better to know what I'm writing down." I keep eye contact. Zeke blinks and shrugs, then keeps writing.

The shark hangs in the water on the left side of the boat. Michael stands just above the shark, drawing the camera around it. I hover two feet from Michael, my notebook clutched to my chest. Without turning away from the shark, he says, "It's like she wanted to get tagged." She—after all that talk yesterday of sisters and how much bigger they are. Bite Size has got four feet on her, easy. "Why is she so small?" I whisper. Michael shakes his head, "I don't know." Again, seeing a shark has made his voice hoarse, his body almost shaking with excitement. He seems literally moved, as though his heart's been squeezed. "I've never met her before," he tells me. "She's new."

His camera slides through the water. The shark makes slow circles around our boat. The actual tag is small against her flank. I search for its shape and then I lose it again. What happens to the data if a sharks swallows and digests a tag? Like Michael told me, the tags don't hurt—the sharks are used to plastic, metal, bones. When I find Michael's face again, I don't know if I am decoy or shark.

I start talking to Zeke at night instead of willing myself not to exist. I learn things about him. He has two parents, a dad and a mom, he is the older brother to two sisters, nineteen and seventeen, he grew up in Oregon, if he weren't studying marine biology, he'd be a Political Science major, and his name is short for Ezekiel. His family is from Palestine and he's Jewish. I say, "Me too, sort of. Jewish, I mean."

Half-Jewish for me or maybe whole-Jewish because it's one mom out of two. (Blake was Jewish and Erin grew up Catholic. Now there's nothing after death for Blake, whereas Erin still wants to believe). Zeke laughs. What's nice about bunk beds is that you can successfully avoid someone's face, if not their body.

"What kind of Jewish are you?" Zeke asks.

"Not very. One of my moms grew up really Jewish. Her parents were Orthodox when she was a kid, but like, modern. We grew up with some of the events, none of the God. I didn't get a bar mitzvah or anything." I realize I was supposed to say bat mitzvah. In the space between my words and when he will correct me, we are two Jewish boys in a bunk bed in a family of men. Salty and dirty, lying in the dark.

But he doesn't correct me. I ask Zeke if he liked it, his bar mitzvah. Not the glow sticks and middle school dance part, but the preparation, reading the Torah, learning to read or at least memorize Hebrew, picking your passage. He says he hated it, actually, the rabbi taught him the passage by phonetics. He didn't have new words, he just had weird fragments of sounds that never added up to anything except being right or wrong.

"I want it to be me," he says. "Who decides it's important, meaningful, whatever. Not someone else."

I scratch my ankle with my socked big toe, and the bed creaks. The windows to our room are dark, slicked with drops of rain. The blankets smell like my stink, salt water, dirt, and fish. Then Zeke mumbles and I can't understand him, and the blankets rustle and the wood creaks from him turning onto his side to sleep.

I fall asleep on my back when my eyes grow too tired to follow the shadow designs across the ceiling.

I'm the first one in the kitchen in the morning. There's a cup left in the sink: a red mug, the dried-out tea bag clinging to its side. I try to lift it and the bottom sticks. I have to wiggle and then pull; the mug comes free with a loud sound like a suction cup. I'm trying to keep things clean, but the smell stays, and objects like these that attach themselves to the spaces I attempt to maintain.

At some point Zeke slides down the stairs, squinting from sleep. Captain emerges from the hallway, demanding coffee. Michael hasn't shown yet. I heat butter in a pan to scramble eggs; we are running out of butter. Zeke sees me scrambling eggs and asks me to count him in. I feel a flush of validation. No toast for him today. My food. Same team. I'm no longer afraid of fucking up. I want to impress. I want to feed this weird family and I want the credit for it, too.

There's a sound at the front door. Michael appears as if out of nowhere at the front step, and stays outside while he bends over to knife the mud out of his boots. His cheeks are pink, his brow hidden underneath a beanie.

There's another sound, bright and bouncing, bringing my attention back inside. Zeke's computer registers the first pop-up tag has hit the surface, and he reacts to the news with his body—his back straightening, hands pushing back hair, fighting a smile. He stares into the screen.

Then, he frowns. His shoulders sink down to where they used to be.

"What's wrong?"

"Tag failure. It's not reporting any data. It should start right when it surfaces."

I sip my coffee. Zeke bites his bottom lip, closes his software, and clicks back in.

"Well, that means you're on retrieval duty today." When he lets me check the screen, the tag throws out a glowing circle, registering blips on an old-school radar. Michael finally enters, a gust of cold and wet wind following him. Zeke calls him over, Michael pulls off his hat and tussles his hair as he assesses the same problem. After they confer for a few moments, they reach a conclusion.

Today we head out on the boat to extract, not give. We have to move fast because pop-up tags can get lost—tangled in seaweed, crushed against rocks, pushed against their flotation into the current and back down to where we can't reach. We want to reach. Captain, Michael, and I drain our coffees and pack up fast and march across the island. It's foggy today, so much so that my clothes feel wet. We are pushing through water to reach more of it.

Captain is excited today, making jokes and grinning, doing an extra sort of dance when he hooks us into the crane and we lower down. Standing at the side railing, I could reach out and touch the island's rock wall. A wave rushes up and smashes, curling into the rock and jumping up at the bottom of the boat. The whitest parts can't reach us, though, and the water falls back to rejoin itself. As the tide surges back, the way the islands continue underwater is revealed: mountainous rock continuing down and down. My hair is up and I packed a sandwich. No forks. Michael isn't looking at me all that much, but feeds me steady instructions for what's about to come.

I press our radio receiver to my cheek with directions from Zeke, which I relay to Captain. Michael tells me that Captain will get us close. "Past Mussel Flat. Through Mirounga Bay." Michael tells me that first to see the tag yells it out. Zeke's voice: "Nearly in West End Cove, but not super inland. It's on the move." Michael tells me that when the second one of us spots it, take out the net. "You're getting close." Michael asks me if I have good grip on the net. "Keep your eyes on the water." Michael asks me again if I've got hands on the net. I like when he tells me what to do but does it by asking questions. "Captain can help."

The water is blue and steel, hard and soft, shifting layers of granite. We're moving through Mirounga Bay to West End, the island Michael left, the more rugged. The narrow channel of water that separates it from ours is filled with rushing, wild currents, not a calm barrier, but an active one. Two small rocks protrude up, other-worldly gates, and we curve around the corner, guided by Zeke and my voice transferring his directions to us. As we lean into the turn, a wave crashes into the rock, ricocheting back over us. My left side gets soaked. I grip tighter to the net.

West End is less green, more desert, its peaks higher and steeper, its bird sounds louder and its smells grosser. Its sides are not flattened off into the ocean but slashed, like several hands spreading their fingers into the water. Captain gets us to the entrance to a large cove, which separates out a triangle of rough water. On land, I see seals, my first clear look at them, fuzzy and barking bodies resting in piles and in stacks, higher up on the rocks than I thought possible. Everything yelling.

Captain declares that he can take a dive for the tag but the ocean might kill him if he tries. I find my hands and I get them on the net. We enter the cove as though it were a clearing—for a second it's calm, as if we've stopped on solid ground—then the waves rush in and crash out and the boat lurches along with it, Captain running the motor hard to fight. The sound of water mixes with the engine, different ends of a sonic register. There are too many water sounds, fragments of fragments filling the air. The consistent rumbling of the motor is never left by itself.

I remember: my moms' house is quiet. At night I could see their faces reflected in an orange rectangle in my window—an image of their bathroom, the two of them moving around at night, the tops of their heads popping into frame, with bickering, teeth-brushing, hair-drying, eyebrow tweezing, loving, medicine retrieving, and turning the lock twice on the cabinet. Erin keeps her jewelry in a bathroom drawer, in an old plastic ice tray, baby blue. Some of the earrings are clip-on. Blake didn't wear jewelry except for a single necklace that her mom had given her, a thick and woven silver chain.

My stomach hurts.

"Spotted!"

Captain's voice yells, the edges gravelly. Zeke in my ear says look, says confirm sighting. The water is foam after crash. I wait for the bubbles to die down, to dissolve, to run to the side. There's an orange light that blinks, pushed against the side of a rock, floating out then thrown back.

My voice makes the second spot. Michael makes third.

"Good job," the voice in my ear says.

Michael smiles—I feel it then. An embarrassing rush that clips me at the ears. My knees push up from my seated position as I move to the edge, where Captain is. Captain's going to get us closer. He tells me to keep the tag in my sights. He doesn't want us too close, though, because then the tide beats the motor and we crash against the rock. There's no crane on this island, no people, no old house, no ghost house. Can I get a couple yards out of my throw? I nod, chin down, hard.

I start to feel the agreement between the water and our boat. There's an invisible line where the push is too hard to resist, as if we're getting run off a treadmill. The boat is an arm and we're reaching for the thing we've dropped down the side of the bed, squeezing our arm into the space between bed and wall, hurting our bones, pushing until skin is red, fingertips scraping at the ground for grip.

The tag bobs above the water and the orange makes a small sun in Michael's eye. My arms move in a U through the air. The line whistles through my palm and I hold on tight to the end. As we pull in the tag, the motor yells, and Zeke yells over that to make sure I hear him: "Confirm tag when retrieved. Retrieved?"

The sun slips out of Michael's pupil. The tag is in my hands, wet and rubbery and slimy. Something born.

"Good work."

Michael kicks the motor again and we make a wave of our own as we speed away from the rocks. My hair is wet, my hands are wet, my body is shaking.

I ask: "What about the other one?"

"Other what?"

"The other tag."

Michael considers. "We should get about a week out of that one before it releases. Hopefully we won't have to come out and get it."

We make it home. When Zeke plugs the tag into his computer, he lets me watch as the program downloads the data: recordings of water depth, light level, temperature, salinity, all measures of the water the shark passed through and when. He also tells me these tags have accelerometers built in, a meter that tracks when and by how much the shark accelerated. It's not data I can understand just by looking at it—another language.

"Huh," Zeke says. He looks around for Michael and Captain, but they're not in the room. I'm jealous of his ability to instantly see meaning in these numbers. "There are two anomalies here," he explains. "One, depth—the shark—what'd you name it?"

"Margo."

"Margo?"

"After Dydek. The tallest pro woman basketball player ever. It's funny 'cause the shark was so small—"

"Oh my god, okay, Margo was swimming at a shallow depth, probably feeding around the islands, when she descended, very quickly, to nearly three thousand feet." He clicks through to the accelerometer data. "That drop corresponds with a huge, like crazy huge, acceleration."

"Can you tell, from looking at that, if the shark was scared?"

Zeke laughs but considers the question. He describes fear as a biological response with several behaviors, one of which is fleeing. Fear is a biological response—revolutionary. Is he going to start quoting *Dune*? Why is he irritating me? I want answers from him, but I want them to be good enough, and when his answers aren't satisfying, I resent the fact that I asked and his position above me. As grad student, as older, as man.

He goes on. This intense change in depth and acceleration could indicate an encounter with an animal bigger than the shark—but the white shark only has a few predators. If we knew this dive was following a specific encounter with one of those mythical bad guys, yes, we could say the animal registered a threat. In general, he says, it's not good to assign emotions to animals. We, unlike them, can see ourselves, giving us the ability to tell stories that explain behavior by way of emotional response.

I don't know how clearly I can see myself.

Who escaped who? Was it a shark, escaping the creature that could eat it? What about a sea lion, narrowly out-swimming a shark? The shark misses its breach, its teeth glaring in the open air, flopping onto itself. The sea lion slips away, using the broken ocean as its cover. The sea lion of my mind crosses to another rock of the Farallons, where it stops and stays put. Maybe it beaches itself. The sea lion squishes itself in between the bodies of its colony. The sea lion finds the highest rock. It makes loud sounds as it runs away.

If I think the shark was scared and Zeke doesn't, what's true? Suddenly comfortable is a world in which behavior is just behavior—unemotional facts. Margo accelerated as she dove. The light levels in the water were high, when the water was shallow, and then low, the deeper she got. I can't see myself any more than that—what happened, what I did, and what happened next. Where's my accelerometer? And if there was a data collecting device attached to me, one that could report dramatic shifts in me and my environment, would it end up changing me too?

Michael left without saying where he was going. I wash the dishes and Zeke dries. His elbows move in small circles in front of his body. The sink water is cold—back at my moms' house, I could lose my hands in hot water and soap, doing enough to not be asked to do anything more. I ask Zeke where Michael went and he tells me, "The lighthouse." Then, "He's got a TV set-up in there. He says it's the fastest WiFi point on island but I think sometimes he needs a break from us." I hand Zeke a large metal pot.

I haven't been to the lighthouse yet. What does it look like inside? I could see a small TV, a folding chair, a battery-powered lantern, maybe an old sofa, nothing too soft because it'd be sure to mold. I fill in the room, adding furniture, bird shit, a spider or two, then Michael, who sighs and cracks his neck before turning on the TV.

"What does he watch?"

"Basketball."

I bet Michael gets up and paces when the game is close. Maybe he shouts at the screen. Warriors fan? Or some team from where he grew up? I don't know where he grew up. I haven't ever heard him raise his voice. I run my finger over a chip in the same red mug that I unstick from the sink. I have discovered it's Michael who likes this cup. He picks it from the shelf I return it to every morning— a silent hand-off, our daily trade. It must be hard to avoid the chip when drinking; maybe his lip fits itself into the cut triangle, inviting its roughness. If he moves slowly, deliberately, nothing hurts. I fill his mug with suds and let them slip slowly out. Then comes the cold water—rinse with as little water as possible, shake the wet off, hand the cup to Zeke.

Zeke finishes his drying duties messily. I can see the water gathering between the plates he stacks before placing them in their cupboard. Wiping his hands on his jeans, he says he's tired. He puts his fist out to bump mine and I make contact and he says he's going to bed, then disappears up the stairs. In that moment he feels like a brother—he uses our familiarity to excuse himself, to make it OK that he did a bad job.

This is my least favorite time, when everyone decides their night is over and I'm still standing. The work's been tiring enough to speed me past this moment into sleep so far, but today there's a nagging energy, inexhaustible. I wander around the living room, looking for items of interest on the walls, in the spines of the books collecting dust on shelves. There's an anchor—classic—and a bright colored flag I don't recognize. Framed photos of old researchers and what this place looked like then. Michael's not back yet. Maybe I'll stay up until he's made it home safely. I try sitting but I'm too anxious. I try reading as I pace, an old sailor's account of the islands from 1897. It says the

Farallons are the top of an underwater mountain range. What we see, what we live on, are the peaks of these mountains.

Finally, Michael reappears, opens the door like he always does. Shoulders rounded, his boots in his hands. I feel instant relief. Validation, too, that I was here for his return home.

"Who won?"

"Warriors. Went to OT. Just preseason."

I go to boil water for tea, ask him if he wants some. He nods, smiles with his lips closed. The pot makes a low rumble as I come back to sit across from him at the table. We sit in silence for a while. Michael's hair is wet, hanging around his face. His wet gives him the impression of clean, but I know it's just the result of trekking through the fog. I am getting so gross that I'm starting to believe an ocean swim could help.

"So, what will you study at Berkeley?" Michael breaks the quiet. I rub my hands and there's grime. What if I just stepped into the ocean and scrubbed?

"I don't know. I was planning on biology, to do pre-med."

Michael's face opens slightly at the eyebrows. "You want to go to medical school?"

"I did. I thought I'd be a good surgeon?"

"Why do you say it like a question?"

"I don't know if that's true anymore. I've jammed my fingers so many times in basketball that they shake." I hope he doesn't look at my hands now, to find the places where the middle joints are swollen and the tips are crooked. "Plus, I hear surgeons are psychopaths."

Michael laughs quietly. "You have to compartmentalize very tough stuff." He pauses. "The young women Julian brings around rarely have that kind of guts. I was relieved, meeting you."

"Thank you," I manage. I want to change my face so that he sees someone different. I want to hold onto my version, where I am another boy in his house—not the girl associated through a connection to his son. I don't like being reminded of Julian here, and in this moment, I decide to tell Michael the truth, "You know, Julian and me, we—"

Michael says, "You don't have to tell me anything he wouldn't tell me. It's okay." His palm flashes through the air in a friendly way, the red and pink that run through its wrinkles. I wonder, then, just how close Michael is to Julian. How much Julian has ever told him. Julian is a good liar. When we first met, he sold fake IDs to me and Tasia and convinced us to pay way too much for them. I'd never drunk and wanted to start, a desire that went against Erin's one major rule for me.

I change direction and ask Michael if he ever misses his family out here. He says of course. "This was the first time Julian was going to see the islands—I was disappointed, when he couldn't. I just hope we'll get another chance." Is he worried about Julian, left sick at home? Did Julian go to his mom's? I realize I don't know. Michael scratches his nose. "It's hard because, you know, I'm not with his mom anymore. Julian splits his time between us, and then I split my time between him and here."

The water boils. I grip the handle of the pot and fill two mugs with hot water. The air smells warm and slightly moldy. I put the mug of tea down in front of him and the cup makes a sound as it collides with the wood. He runs his finger around the rim. Leans down, blows into the steam. I return to my spot across from him and do the same with my tea. In the corner of the room is the staircase, which leads to the second floor, which holds our bedrooms. Does he sleep in a bunkbed? Does he share space with Captain, changing when Captain's out of the room? Or he sleeps alone, in a mysterious adult bedroom, where he throws his jeans over his desk chair and slides into a queen bed.

I ask him about the nature of his work—there's no office, no clear rules. Is there stability? Does that matter to him? I'm asking, obviously, because I don't know if I want to be a surgeon and I don't know what else I'm supposed to do. Could I survive like this? Working like he does? I don't say all of this out loud.

Steam wafts up around his chin and nose. He tells me that, no, this job isn't stable. Like an artist's life, it's project to project, where much of your energy goes into the searching in between: for the next place, the next research, the next grant that will make the work possible. That can be stressful, all the work that goes into wanting-to-work. You have to want it badly. As for the rules, though, he feels there are rules, and they make more sense to him in this world. "They are not arbitrary," he tells me. "They're what we know about the natural world and how not to fuck it up. It's rational and it's humbling to respond to what's literally around you."

"I understand that," I tell him.

Blake's work started with her hands and I thought mine would too. I had good, quick hands, strong fingers, and I like intensity.

I like fixing things. Surgery is all of that. It's a good job, and from what I've heard, an all-consuming one. You make good money. You work a ton. You walk close to people's pain and try to take it away from them.

"I'm so sorry about your mom," he says.

A cold wash goes over my head, starting right at the roots of my hair. He isn't supposed to know that about me, but, of course, he does—I spent all that time at his house over the summer, and even though Julian was constantly avoiding him, trying to finagle space without parents, I was always hoping he'd be there when we got home.

Michael reaches and grabs my knee, tugging it inches toward him, holding my kneecap between two fingers. His handle on me makes me aware of my bones. I want to pinch his fingers, to take his hold into my hand and squeeze. He squeezes then, fingers pressing, and then releases. Julian never listened to me that thoroughly—he often told me it wasn't that deep. He couldn't take me seriously.

Michael says he's going to take his tea to bed and thanks me. Quieted, I say, "Me too," and I walk behind him as if I've been instructed to move in single file. The back of his head is slick again from the fog. When we reach the top of the stairs, I go left and he goes right. Instead of looking back, he lifts his mug into the air. There are his broad shoulders, his strong back, his butt in his jeans, the bare ankles and weathered heels. There is his body as he walks away. I can't avoid how he's changing to me.

Part of me walks into his room, into the dark, where the edges of my body dissolve. He sits in a rolling chair and I put my head on his knee, where his hand moves to brush my hair off my forehead. There, his eyes open into mine, my chin into his muscle, and he asks: "What do you want?" Heat rushes the back of my neck in a spinal line.

There I am at my doorway. My body itches to follow my boss into the dark. I don't.

I follow my routine. I am a decoy-prepper, line-thrower, talker-into-radio. I move fast and I boil eggs for no less than seven minutes and no more than eight and a half. What matters on this island is time. I keep everyone fed without wasting it. When we run out of eggs, I make oatmeal. When we run out of oats, I leave the dry foods that we have on the kitchen table and clean the sink. Real science. I'm so happy I'm good at what I do. I didn't know you needed good hands, a tough nose, delicate ears, and an outside body to do this work. I was worried I wasn't going to be smart enough. I was worried I wouldn't have the right mind.

Zeke stays back most days on the computer to build our data archive. This isn't a job where I'd want to get promoted, because then I'd be more with the computer and less with the fish, water, salt, risk. Less with the world. Zeke still gets to find high ground in the afternoons to scan for attacks. His absence means Michael wants me taking more notes, filling those complicated data sheets he slips into his notebook.

This morning, I wake up and it's sunny. I go downstairs and Captain's not at the table. Michael—of the hallway, of the upstairs bedroom—reports that Captain's sick. He's sleeping it off in his room. I can't picture Captain sick enough not to work—he acts like he's never missed a chance to labor in his life—but Michael's face and tone make it fact.

It's just us today.

I wait for Michael to smile, to ask me questions about the weather and the day, to poke at me with his little jokes and encouragements, but his face is somber, tired. His eyes are red, his cheeks and upper neck somewhat swollen. He's quiet. His quiet makes me jittery, wanting to rouse in him how he normally acts around me.

My family friend Frank, a longtime friend of my moms, was always grumpy except when he was in the ocean or doing a cross-word puzzle. He had long hair and a handlebar mustache that reached past where his face ended. Blake thought that I flirted with him when I was little. She chalked it up to my lack of a father. They were fancier than we were, Frank's family, and owned a beach house on the east coast that we went to some summers.

At night Frank sat in the corner doing crossword puzzles while his wife cooked dinner. Sometimes he took his canoe out and rowed until after the sun had set. I remember the acrid smell of bug spray, the salt of meat and grease on the grill, how the pink Calamine lotion dried crusty on my mosquito bites. My legs were pink polka dots, my arms sticky with bug killer. Frank's daughter, who was my age and a bitch, found out she had Lyme disease the day after we'd run through the marsh behind their house, cattails crawling with bugs.

It moves quick, I thought. She cried and cried but it wasn't chronic and soon got fixed—Frank brought her a bowl of ice cream and rubbed her back until she felt better.

Blake said it was hard to describe, the way I changed when he entered a room, the way I talked myself up. It was like watching someone else's daughter. I don't remember feeling any way about Frank, except that the rough hairs of his mustache were fun to tug at, and Erin swears it wasn't like that. I grew up with two moms but I did not grow up in a world in which men didn't exist.

Before there were established places to freeze and share sperm, lesbians recruited gay men to have their babies or they went to two-room clinics on college campuses where tall and attractive college boys would do their thing in one room and pass it over, still warm, to the next room. My moms were part of the first wave at the California Cryobank. My moms kept my donor's file, which included substantial but non-identifying information, but didn't let me read it, instead parsing out the details over time. Like a slow and too-loaded bedtime story. My donor went to Stanford, was six foot four and a half, had a 4.0 GPA at time of donation, and blue eyes. Physics major. Swim team. Favorite food: chicken-fried steak.

Michael peels an orange, his eyes fixed out the window. The scratching buzz of a radio transmission breaks my thinking. Michael springs up, leaving the fruit split open, its peel curling off into a half-spiral. He speaks into the radio receiver. As the response crackles back, his face expands. "There's been an attack," he tells me. A friend of Michael's on a nearby sailboat saw blood in the water, a large fin, and splashing. Lots of it.

The sun draws lines into the kitchen. The kitchen is never as bright as it is today. We're going to the site of an attack. I don't really know what that means. Zeke's face finds me. His eyes flashing, he's quietly jealous. He has more video footage to scrub on the computer. He's tied to the inside today. Jealousy is the mark of a real friend. I grin wide at him. The first reported attack of our trip, and I get to see it.

Michael and I march down to the crane. We lower ourselves into the water. The blonde-gray hairs stand up from the back of his neck. When he un-hooks us from the crane, he turns to me and calmly demands: "Talk me through our approach." I don't understand. His voice creaking, he says: "I need you to drive the boat."

"Why?"

His eyes flutter, impatient. Irritated that I am asking why. He clears his throat. His face pale.

"Are you feeling alright?"

"Do you not think you can do it?"

"No, of course I can do it. I just—"

"Good." I think about trees, sunshine, a dog asleep in a patch of sun. My therapist taught me to visualize scenes of calm when I'm feeling anxious. Sometimes I think of the ocean, but the ocean is here, and it is not calm. Michael rolls his head in a circle around his neck, wincing as he goes.

He instructs me to drive the boat—he believes I can do it. So I can do it. Right? This time I am Zeke's radioed voice. To Michael I talk through our approach: north from East Landing, past Shubrick Point, curve around to North Landing. The attack took place in Fisherman's Bay, the bay contained just above where we've been stationed before. To myself, in my head: drive calmly enough so that I don't scare the sea lions, drive slowly enough so that I don't run them over. To Michael, out loud: "Ready to cut the motor when you make first spot."

Michael nods. "Good."

"Good," I repeat.

The islands are a different place in the sun. Colors are brighter. We can see birds in the sky from farther away. We can see the bridge with its bronze legs in the ocean. The breeze is welcome, the cold is welcome, and the water seems nearly livable. Up above us, at North Landing, there is a small building—a solid-colored rectangle, not much taller than me, with a slit just below its flat-top roof. The slit could fit part of a person's face, maybe. A hearty package. It's the blurry line of a mail slot from far away. I have no idea what the building is for—extra supplies? A refuge for the birds?

The motor rumbles underneath me. I don't need to keep my hand clutched on the throttle—it holds its place, once set—but it makes me feel more in control. When Michael yells, "Spot!" I cut the engine, my eyes moving quickly to find the attack on the horizon. My perspective swells and falls with the waves. There is a hunk of animal in the water about forty yards from us. Around the carcass the water is pinkish red, something spilled.

Michael spins his head around. "Start the motor up again, softer this time. We can get closer."

I don't see any shark fins; whatever did this has left the scene.

It doesn't mean they won't be back.

"We've done this before, Captain and I," he says, explaining somewhat impatiently. "Sharks aren't bothered when we're around them feeding. We're sure to see scavengers on the scene soon enough. It won't matter where we are."

I restart the motor. The boat crawls closer. Nearing ten yards, Michael tells me to cut it again. I do, and the sound stops, and it's as quiet as it gets out here. Chunks of whitish yellow foam float around the body, which Michael identifies as seventy-five to one hundred pounds left of an elephant seal. The whitish yellow is fat.

I fell at a crowded party over the summer and collided with a wine bottle, glass which broke on its way down and pierced the crease of my right arm. I was so drunk I didn't feel the slicing, only the sensation of blood moving rapidly out. I'd never been that drunk before, so drunk that my pain was redacted, erased as the blood left my body. I stepped up, looked down, and saw bone through the mangled mix of muscle, tendon, and blood. At the hospital, they gave me a painkiller before they stitched me up, but I didn't need it. Erin protested—she's very drunk—and I protested— I wanted to watch—but the nurse insisted I shouldn't be awake for the stitches. I woke up and I'd been put into one piece again. I asked Erin what my arm was like when the wound was cleaned. She told me that for a skinny girl, my arm was mostly fat. Like a layer cake with too much frosting.

I imagine picking up the hunks of yellow-white blubber and padding my body with it, inflating my arms and legs.

The boat rocks next to the blood and the body. Michael jots down notes, muttering to himself. His bloodshot eyes dart up and scan the edges of what we can see—above us, the land, the rock gravely and chippy where the grass runs out, the mystery building. To our far right, the smaller islets and rocks in a clump, some of them obscured by the curving edge of the island wall directly next to us. Then back to the blood. I try to find the elephant seal's face, its tell-tale nose, the eyeballs hidden behind wrinkled skin. There's nothing. Only a large, rounded mass with jagged ends, the skin peeling back from different bites. The loose and floating bits of skin are pulpy like wet paper.

My arm healed slowly. Erin was furious with me. She didn't let me take the hydrocodone, gave me extra strength Tylenol in its place. Over and over again, she asked me: Don't you know our family? Haven't you seen how drinking and using have hurt us? Don't you understand what's at risk? Every time Erin got mad at me for my arm, or for anytime that I drank, I heard it as a plea: You're at risk of becoming Mom. Don't. It was as if the worst outcome for me had already been decided and it was my job to avoid it at all costs. I didn't want to accept this fate, or to believe I had one in the first place. Erin didn't get why I'd started drinking after swearing I wouldn't for so long. I couldn't explain it to her, and she wasn't able to convince me—or ground me—away from my new and deep stubbornness.

Michael's eyes get caught where they are—up. A shark approaches from the west, a dark-gray mass with sharp fin, fully intact. Pressure fills my chest. The shark closes the distance between us in seconds. We are so close. My stomach a solid block.

.The teeth make a thousand pearls when the shark breaks the surface. White sharks have five rows of teeth that are always growing, replacing themselves forever. The rows of teeth look wrong, raw, ordered but mismatched, like an assembly of wounds. Flesh falls away from the body as the shark disappears under the water with its food.

Michael turns then. We stand farther apart than I thought we stood. His jaw is slack, eyes gooey, all exhale. He is so happy. He smiles his first smile of the entire day. Maybe he caught Captain's bug, a lighter version of it. "I know this shark," he says. "Angela." Our laughter starts in unison. "Angela?" I repeat, disbelieving. No way he's one of those pet owners who names his dog a too-human name, like Ronald, Deborah, Edward, Angela. "It's a long story," he says. "Wish we could get another tag on her."

There are researchers that place long-term tags on sharks, but Michael's not one of them—his tags are pop-off, meaning, we place them, they ride with the sharks for a few days, up to a week, and then the tag releases, giving us the data when it hits the surface. Our main goal is to chart the population here, not see where the sharks migrate to afterwards. If we're able to tag the same sharks multiple years in a row, we get valuable data about their behavior when passing through these feeding grounds.

The breeze pushes a piece of hair into my eye, and it's a sharp, quick pain. I blink, eyes watering. He looks away. He's trying to protect me, not embarrass me. I blink until it doesn't hurt anymore, grateful for what feels like privacy.

Then I see he's looking at something.

Two shapes, huge, bigger than white sharks, darker, too, blue-ish black, with black fins and patches of white at their front. One fin is curled over, floppy, lackluster. They're not far enough from us. Twenty yards? One hundred? Scale is gone with time.

There's a large dark shape in front of them. The shark that just fed and swam away.

Two orcas herd a white shark. Angela. She races away, fast. Michael says, "Run the motor." In front of us: the shark and orcas. Behind us: the island wall. I don't know if he wants us to escape or to declare that we are here or both.

In that famous documentary about orcas in captivity, a Sea World trainer is tugged underwater, her foot in the orca's jaws. Her body becomes a blurry shape stuck at the bottom of the pool, her hair floating upward. On Discovery Channel's Shark Week, ominous orchestral music fills moments like the one we're actually inside. I run the motor. "Switch with me," he says. I scramble off the controls and to the front, where I have a better view.

Michael goes to grab the throttle and steering wheel. He moves not with Captain's hands, but his own, and the boat moves as I pulse with a feeling between excitement and terror. He tells me that when orcas attack white sharks, they go for the liver. A white shark's liver means six hundred pounds of meat. He tells me this act of predation is very rare. His voice is the type of quiet and calm that only surfaces in a crisis.

He gets us out of the direct path of the orcas, but he keeps us close enough to observe. Both of us in the front, peering over the railing. He asks for his journal and pencil. I give it to him. Number 2 of 5. He tells me I need to write too. Be as specific as I can. I'm not brave, what I'm feeling is fear, and I want to do like the sea lions do and find land. The other part of me, curious and moving and slippery, wants to look and keep looking.

The orcas cut off Angela as she tries to escape. The larger whale throws its body on top of her and Angela's fin dips beneath the water. Angela slows, nearly stops. Instead of racing the other direction, she curls into a turn, swimming in a tight, steady circle. The orcas trace the same circle around her, spiraling for several minutes until the larger of the two finally moves to stop her, to cut her off before she can tuck into a shape out of their reach. There is no biting—just slamming, ramming, slapping with its fins. Angela slows, sinks. One of the orcas comes up from beneath her and lifts her, with its whole body, Angela ascending to the surface, now on her back, white flesh facing the sky.

Michael tells me that white sharks enter a state known as tonic immobility when on their backs for too long—a trance state.They become disoriented. They freeze. They're unable to move. More time passes. The time hurts. Some sharks, white sharks included, must swim constantly in order to breathe. They get oxygen as the water rushes through their gills. If they stop moving, they stop breathing. If they stop breathing, they die.

One of the orcas suddenly makes a move for Angela's side, her lower abdomen. Biting her. There is a small rush of blood in the water. I want to hold onto Michael. The orca makes a quick circle and rams into Angela on her other side, squeezing a substance out of the wound the size of an orca's head, a large and misshapen oval. It's a lighter pink than blood, disintegrating into the water. The liver. I hear a high-pitched cry, a celebratory whining. One of the orcas whistling, a sound so clear and bright it cuts into my forehead. The other orca slides around Angela, joining its friend, and their jaws open and close around the liver. Eating it.

After the liver is gone, the orcas are gone too. Angela's body sinks. I thought it might float, but she drops until I can't find her anymore—her outline made cloudy until the dark ocean takes her. The ocean is momentarily silent. Michael pants, writing furiously, his journal pressed against the flat of his knee, his weather-proof pants hiked up the calves. He sweats. I try to write too.

In middle school I dissected sheep lungs for a week because I had a science teacher who thought we should see inside a body larger than a frog. The lamb lungs, as Tasia called them, exaggerating the *b* and *ng* sounds, drawing them out in her mouth, were spotted and gray. They did not seem all the way dead—when I cut into them, the split flesh sighed and expanded. Because they weren't part of any official lesson plan, and because it was optional, there was no charted route in. Our teacher encouraged me to cut and find whatever I wanted to, the point was to experiment. There were several sets of lungs and for three days in a row they were available to us. After day two, Tasia leaned over and whispered that the smell was sticking to me.

The scalpel our teacher gave me was incredible, its sharpness unbelievable. The damage it did, it did softly, the blade sliding deep without resistance. I cut so excitedly that the lungs were a mash of gray by the end of the class, minced rubber. I was disappointed in myself. Destroying didn't feel good. I wanted to be more precise. I wanted to find a shape on the inside that I couldn't see from the surface.

"We're a part of a very special natural event, Lydia," Michael says. "This hasn't happened here in ten years. It rarely ever happens."

We end up climbing into the middle of the boat, our backs against the console with the controls, our butts on the boat floor, where we compare notes. At some point I write: "Angela sinks. Belly up— she's so pale. Really sad. All of liver gone." And Michael reaches over and puts his hand over mine. There's his pulse pushing from his wrist. We are sharing a feeling, and a closeness, its shaky edges running through the both of us. Maybe I am a conduit for a particular kind of electricity. Maybe he is too.

His fingers slip around my palm until they grab the meaty part under my thumb. He's after my bones again. What if I want his? What if I reach into his abdomen and take a piece of the liver?

I kiss Michael. He tastes sour. I taste sea water. I taste blood. I am not sinking but floating; I am not floating but swimming.

Back at the house, I take off my shoes slowly, pulling the backs from my heels, holding it in. Inside me is expanse. Michael knocks his heels against the door frame, sending dirt flying instead of methodically removing the mud with a knife like he normally does. Strands of hair pull away from his face. The sky is dark outside. The wind is low. Part of me wants to stay outside, so that nothing changes, so that everything we saw and experienced stays there. On the boat ride back, Michael's hands started to shake so I drove again.

I am happy, so happy I'm almost drunk with it, and I want to know if he feels the same. He didn't recoil from the kiss—he leaned in. For several seconds I was close enough to him to feel the insides of his lips, the softest parts.

Inside, Zeke is waiting, sitting at the kitchen table, his face casual and curious. He offers a congratulatory remark: "Your first attack."

"Actually, we saw two," I correct him, and my voice makes two too pronounced, revealing that one must be different than the other, we saw one and then—heavy metal voice—two. I saw the second! I could say too much, it could all fall out of me if I'm not careful. I smile with my lips hiding my teeth. Zeke is confused and asks me again, and I tell him we saw two killer whales murder a white shark. "We saw them do the liver thing, and then the shark just sank, like, they didn't even eat her body!" I exhale, waiting for his reaction, letting my teeth take their place in my grin. I feel like a wild animal, my body betraying me. But Zeke is quiet. "You're sure?"

"I saw it. It happened—" Pointing across the room. "—there!" A shudder moves through me, the adrenaline not done, not worn.

"Are you serious?" He stands now, alarmed. "Do you know what this means?"

I don't. I was looking forward to Zeke's jealousy, the salty sting of his bitter admiration. The door opens. Michael comes inside now, dropping his boots. Zeke touches his index finger to his thumb and breathes deeply through his nose, releasing his fingers as he breathes out.

"The sharks leave," Zeke says on an exhale.

"What?"

"The sharks leave," repeats Michael. "We had shark season here ten years ago. We didn't see the attack, but we were tracking the sharks, of course, we had already gotten a great sense of the population over years of being here. We knew them." Zeke told me it was wrong to make animals into characters with emotions, but Michael speaks about them as friends. "When Peggy—she used to run a whale watching tour that got close to the islands—told us what had happened, what someone on her boat had videotaped, badly, of course, we watched as all the sharks left, and didn't come back, some until the following season."

They found that when pods of orcas came close to the islands and stayed, for a matter of hours, the sharks left, some staying gone for an entire year. Once a shark was killed, the presence of the orcas alone was enough to spook them.

I don't want to remember: Erin cleaned out Blake's side of the closet just days after she died, stacking up the old t-shirts, holed sweaters, work pants, and dress shirts, the socks piled in one large lump. There were bras too, some large and underwired, girlier than I ever thought she wore. Erin couldn't get rid of the toiletries, though, the toothbrush and toothpaste, the cheap plasticky comb, the thick wax Blake used to work through her hair.

Will I have to go home? Without the sharks, will they send me home? To toothbrushes that don't take care of teeth? To a grief museum bathroom? I can't fail.

Without sharks, we have nothing to study. Suddenly our predicament strikes me as absurd—all the way out here, where it's difficult to survive, where we must boat in food to keep living, we insist our presence here has a purpose. We want to watch the sharks, tag them, decode their remaining mysteries. Then the sharks leave, because they get scared. And we're still here. The sharks respond to a balance that has nothing to do with us. The ocean doesn't care and the sharks don't either.

Michael's face is a mix of emotions. Sad, stressed, playful, invigorated, excited. He has life back, having made a full recovery from this morning.

"Where's Will?" he asks, and I almost forget who he's talking about, using Captain's real name.

Zeke nods up the stairs. "Sleeping."

"Will you get him for me, please?"

Zeke's head jolts toward me, as if delegating this task to me with his body—she should do it. Michael repeats the question. Zeke clearly wants to self-destruct, but nods and jogs up the stairs, leaving me and Michael alone again, when I hope I will get some answers, a sense of feeling from him, at the very least, but Michael is all business, the wheels in his forehead whirring and spinning.

"Lydia, how many sharks do we have logged now?"

"I—I don't know. I think Zeke said it was around ten, fifteen." Michael nods, his expression descending into something flat, impossible to read. "Okay."

Zeke comes down the stairs with Captain, then, Captain rubbing his temples, his balding hair sweaty and slick by his ears. He looks sick, vulnerable and small. Captain sits while Zeke stays standing, antsy, squeezing his hands. Before Michael talks, he reaches for Captain, holding him, first by the collar and then at the wrist, his gestures surprisingly emotional. The room grows private in the way I hoped for Michael and me. The intimacy between them wants to kick me out.

"A pair of orcas attacked and killed Angela today," Michael tells Captain. "I don't know if it's the same pair from ten years ago or a different pod that has adopted their menu."

Captain jerks and sinks. Captain yelps and exhales. Captain grabs his broken pinky and wiggles it, a clicking sound fills the small space. "Well, fuck."

Captain leans his head forward to rest on Michael's shoulder. Just as he touches down, he springs back up, seeming to remember we are in the room with him. Then a jolt of energy passes through him, as he sizes Michael up and asks, "What was it like?"

"Brutal," Michael says, and his hands shake again.

Julian skips across my brain. How wrong he was, about slow results and hard, boring work. A sick satisfaction fills me, how we saw something he will never see, and how we did something he'd never predict. I am beyond his limiting ideas for me. Meanwhile, Zeke glares at me from across the room, another story, because he could have seen the attack and didn't.

Michael tells us that protocol for the rest of the trip may have to change. If sharks behave according to established patterns, we may stop seeing them. It might not be worth it to boat out every day. Shark watch could move to land, to the lighthouse, the highest point on SEFI. Our data from this summer may be limited, but we have this observed interaction that is incredibly rare, and we get to find out what happens next.

"Maybe this buys us another year here," Michael suggests to Captain. "It's definitely another paper."

Captain sighs, then rubs his knuckles into his temples. "Another loss."

"It could be another isolated event," Zeke says.

"I don't see MARO giving us more money if there are fewer and fewer sharks to study."

"There will always be sharks here," Zeke presses.

"I don't know," says Michael.

I don't fully understand the coded negotiation at play, a mix of grief and optimism, trading forecasts for what this attack can mean, for them, for the islands, for the sharks. If I could insert myself into the history of the relationships here, I could be included in this intimacy, too, instead of feeling as if I'm on the outside of a private family matter. A sense of alienation grows in me, a wall that pushes me away from today's events and how they tied me to Michael.

When Captain finally notices me, he congratulates me for what I saw. Expanding in his attention, I tell him I drove the boat, too, that I tried to mimic how he does it. Captain blinks, a miniscule tick, before muttering, "All right then, kid. Big day," and when he turns back to Michael, it's with an energetic accusation, and Michael gets quiet.

"She did good," Michael pushes back.

"She shouldn't have to."

A bag of trail mix is open on the table, cashews and raisins spilling out.

"What's for dinner?" Zeke asks, breaking the moment. And because I have taken on the cooking, because I wanted them to rely on me without asking me for it, they all turn their heads to me.

When Michael says he's going to bed, part of me moves to follow, but he leaves the table quickly. We kissed! We witnessed a historical event! The contents of the day are hard to contain inside me, I'd like to ask for it over again. I'd like another kiss. I'd like to feel close to him again. I do what is easier but horrible and trudge up the stairs to my room. I sit cross-legged on my bed. The blanket rubs against my knees. When we're in the dark, I ask Zeke if he knew Angela the shark and where her name came from.

"I don't know the full story," he tells me. "It's someone's name, though. Captain picked it."

I replay Captain leaning into Michael, his forehead brushing the fabric of Michael's flannel. Men need crisis and excuses to touch each other. Girls aren't like that. They can hug, squeeze, hold hands, even, and it's part of the language they're given. If I were a boy, would no one touch me? Would I lose something?

Julian was on the wrestling team at his high school and I liked watching him compete. When I asked him to teach me some moves, he went half-strength at first, moving in slow motion around me. When I told him to go one hundred percent, I felt how strong he was, the muscles above a buzzing well of power, and fell into a dream-like state as he moved with me, so that by the time his legs were wrapped around my back, holding my arm by the wrist, pulling me from the shoulder socket, I didn't even know that I was in pain. The feeling flooded in, a fiery line below my left shoulder blade.

I hear Zeke squirm in his bunk below me, the wood squeaking and the blankets rustling.

"Why did you even come here, anyway?" Zeke demands. I can feel the rage emanating from the bottom bunk. "You might wanna be a scientist? What is that?" He can't slow down. His voice trips forward, fast. "I've spent so much fucking time trying to be where you were today by accident. You didn't even want it. How is that fair?"

If we were standing right now, would Zeke take the same tone with me? Would he straighten his spine, tilt his chin up, try to get bigger than me? I'm stronger than he is and I know it bothers him. "How do you know what I want?" I don't have the space to sit up in bed.

"I don't have the connections you do," he says. "I'm not a family friend to anyone important."

I'm quiet. He doesn't know me. Friend of the family? I was just sort-of fucking Michael's son. Why did Michael let me take Julian's place? Because of what he saw in me? Because he pitied me? Because he wanted my bones? Because he wanted to sleep with me?

"We'll probably spend the rest of the season waiting for nothing," Zeke mumbles. Real science.

The next day Michael's not at breakfast. Captain says Michael wants to sit with the data this afternoon, that he went on a morning walk. He wants to stay and he wants to go. Strange. Is his absence because of me? If I had woken up earlier, made it downstairs before the lights came on, could I have seen him, spoken to him? Would he reach for me? Anxiety makes a shut door of my throat.

"Why?" I ask.

"He'll be back," Captain says, ignoring my question. "I'm taking us out today."

I make a porridge with two ancient packets of instant oatmeal I found in the depths of the cupboard, a can of coconut milk, dried nuts, and pumpkin seeds. It smells better than it tastes. Another shipment of food and supplies is supposed to be on its way to us this week, weather permitting. Captain told me about a time that rogue storms delayed their rations by three weeks. By the time the food made it, their diet had been reduced to dry pasta, Diet Coke, and peanut butter.

Zeke, Captain, and I head out to the crane, the boat, the water. Captain whistles as we walk, trying to make bets on what we'll see. "Fifty bucks for nothing," he says. "A hundred?" I counter with bets on sea lions, elephant seals, and seabirds. I throw out random numbers: twelve sea lions, two elephant seals, fifty-five seabirds. Captain chuckles. He won't take those odds. Zeke wears a constant glare. He doesn't laugh, doesn't join in. His bitterness makes me feel closer to him, weirdly, like I've earned a reaction from him. I'm enough to make him see me as competition.

When we walk along the path, I look for Michael. A human body should stick out here. He should be easy to find. But I don't see him, only empty land and birds.

How much has changed in just a few days. What does it mean if the job goes away? What does it mean if, when the sharks stop, we stop? I am already attached: to the days spent on the water, my hands holding the shark decoy, gathering disparate points of data and trying to fill the space between them. The type of tired I am. The type of small I feel when watching orca whales kill a white shark and strip its liver from its body. I want to pray to that death. I want to pray to all animals that make me tiny and unimportant.

Erin says praying is thinking really hard. Then letting go. Whereas Blake would say it's wishful thinking. Then coming back to the real world. I want Blake to come back to the real world. My ankles ache. In the boat, the clouds wash over us. We string out the decoy and wait. The sun moves lower in the sky, giving us long shadows when we stand up and move around the boat. Nothing comes. We feel alone in the water.

Captain asks if we'd like to go for a swim. He'll take us to where he dives for sea urchins, where he knows how to enter the water calmly and quietly, sneaking in next to the sharks by Little Murre Cave. We should experience every piece of this place, and if the sharks really did leave, we've got one less thing to worry about in the ocean. Captain goes so far as to say there's nothing to worry about. This risk diagnosis makes sense coming from Captain, who is also a diver, who knows the proper way to breathe underwater.

Zeke says he doesn't swim, but the way he says it leaves room for convincing. He wants to be asked to swim. He wants to be wanted out loud. I tell Captain yes, if Zeke goes. "Come on," I press Zeke. "Our trip just got so boring." The truth is, I'm not sure anything can match what I've already seen. Zeke presses his lips together, a yes starting on the bottom of his cheeks. I win. He says fine. He pushes his thumb into his index finger. All the men here have ticks with their hands, anxious fingers.

This so-called safe place is just underneath Shubrick Point, en route back to East Landing. The water is calm today, the tide medium low, and the sky a flat sheet of gray. Captain anchors the boat twenty or thirty feet from the entrance to the cave, which is a dark oval into the side of the island's flank. You can tell the tide's low because more island gets revealed, the ocean drops, and the rock and dirt that make up the island stay wet, making for layers of brown, gray, and black. The cave's entrance is half flooded, the top of it visible above the waves, ceilings like watery catacombs, continuing farther back than my eyes think it should.

If we do this, can we say we went swimming with sharks? The idea is to share this water, if only for a short period of time. Shared is the wrong word. We visited the sharks. We walked into their house. We fell into their house when they weren't home.

Captain stops the boat. He turns around, facing us. He breathes in and out in short, deliberate breaths, taking his arms and lifting them up the sides of his body until they are stretched above his head. He nods and widens his eyes, gesturing us to mirror him, showing us how we will hold our breath. The beginning of learning to breathe underwater is a series of breaths on land. We try. We huff and puff along with him, we raise our arms like we are performance artists aligning our bodies to the wind. We try to maintain our balance and our focus. Then Captain allows himself an extended exhale and his hands drop from his head to his waist, to his knees, to the bottom of the boat. He stays there a second. His hands move first, pushing upward, faster this time, as he breathes in, deep and long, a gulp of air as though there's a balloon in his chest. When his chest broadens and his hands are in the air, he stops there. He holds it.

Zeke is in boxers, his bare chest prickling in the exposed air. I'm in running shorts and sports bra. We skipped over the part where we changed in front of each other, now teammates on some weird sports team. If Zeke played basketball, he'd never box out. He'd be obsessed with shot form, running the perimeter only, calling for the ball until he lost his voice.

Captain nods fiercely, excitedly. He brings his arms to his sides and creeps to the back of the boat, where he grips the small ladder next to the engine and mimes lowering himself into the water.

"No splashing," he says. "Gentle. Slow."

I drop down the ladder, and slide into the water before I can make any other choice. For a moment, everything is quiet. I open my eyes to dark blue. The cold rips the saved air out of my lungs. I hear a splash, not my own, telling me that Zeke got in the water too. He didn't follow Captain's warning. Or he fucked up. I resurface gasping.

Captain grins. "Ain't nothing you can do about the temperature."

I can't find Zeke. The water doesn't feel calm, it feels massive and rising. I am small and warm, slowly freezing. I reach for the side of the boat. Its texture, unnatural and plasticky, is comforting. There are sounds gurgling around me. A dark shadow passes underneath my feet. My face meeting the water and the water meeting me, I scream, sending Captain around to my edge of the boat.

"There's something in the water! There's something in the water!"

Captain starts to reach for me, telling me to move, get closer. But as I'm moving, the terror in my body that I have entered a shark's home while it was still present, that I could be eaten, that I am small and consumable—Captain says, "Sea lion." Real calm, his words an even line. "They're just sea lions."

Captain holds my arms as levers and pulleys, not body parts, and suddenly I'm not in the water anymore. It's colder in the air, with the sun leaving, the wind hitting my skin, water sliding from chunks of hair down my neck.

On the other side of the boat, Zeke resurfaces. He spits out salt water and asks, yells, how long was he down there. Then yelps, seeing a dark shape like I did. My eyes refocus slowly on the water that surrounds us. There are many, many sea lions. I've never seen this many in the water together. Swirling, flipping, their whiskers tracing the surface. When their necks lift above the surface, they elongate, becoming cartoon snakes with eyes and whiskers.

"Sea lions!" I yell. Shuddering, Zeke nods. His hair separates into spikes when it's wet. He's brave out here, wanting to be liked but wanting to dive and stay underwater, too. It's enough to make me want to throw myself out of the boat and try again. I force myself to move slowly as I put my clothes back on, to steady my jaw so my teeth don't chatter.

Captain pulls Zeke onto the boat and tells him he did good. Zeke smiles like he did great. The sea lions, now one dark mass in the water, fill what we can see. Captain navigates us through the crowd and we're off, back toward home.

Captain tells us a story about a first date he went on with a woman who worked as a professional diver, diving for treasure, lost items, precious metals, pieces of shipwrecks. Sometimes she dove with an oxygen tank and sometimes she free dove. "Free diving can take ten to fifteen years off your life," Captain tells us, whistling. "She didn't care. Didn't give a single shit."

I ask why free diving makes your life shorter. Captain claims that the repeated pressure to your lungs shrinks them. It's just risky. It's like free soloing. "You see guys in their seventies, climbing mountains with no ropes? No. They've all died off by then."

Obviously their first date was to the ocean. Captain already knew a thing or two about free-diving. He'd started diving for sea anemones with some friends for extra cash, but wasn't experienced like she was. When she dipped under the surface, she disappeared for a long time. Five minutes. Nearly ten sometimes.

"And this first time," Captain says, "She wants to go down with me. After about ten meters we start to sink, there's less oxygen in the water and you start to feel your weight a bit, it gets easier, she's holding my hand, this hot broad, as we're sinking further and further into the ocean. The pressure rises, my ears start to hurt like shit, and she's looking at me and smiling, like she's all fucking good, like it's gonna pass, and I think OK, let it pass, and eventually it does, the water starts to feel like it's flattening you, which makes it easier on your body to function, actually, the pressure changes the chemistry of your blood—"

"It changes your blood chemistry?" I shiver in disbelief. Zeke laughs. "Gases dissolve more easily under that pressure," he explains. "Your spleen spits out extra oxygen into your red blood cells."

Captain continues, "The natural nitrogen in the body starts to work on ya quicker. I didn't know that, then, though, all I know is we're probably at about 30 or 40 meters and I feel drunk, like, fucked up, super happy, smiling at this woman as we keep sinking, but then my lungs start to hurt, and when I'm looking up the sun is getting smaller and smaller through the water, things are getting darker, is it me or is it how deep we are? I tried to bolt. This chick took the hint but slowed me down. Swam with me, slowly, the whole way up. Nearly blacked out but I made it."

"Were you mad?" Zeke asks. "Like, this girl almost got me killed?"

"Ha! No," Captain says, his voice booming. "I was pissed because she stayed calm, and I lost my head. I said I'd never lose my head like that again. And the next time we dove I'd stay down as long as she could."

"Did you?" I ask, shaking less.

"Took me longer than I wanted it to. And then she left. She died a few years back."

A heavy silence settles across the boat. Angela. It has to be. I timidly offer an I'm sorry to Captain, who, growing gruffer by the minute, grunts and brushes it off. Spray crashes into the boat, the water swirling. Staring at Captain's face, trying to understand why he told us the story, wanting to stave off the newly surfaced pain. He wanted to impress her? To be her equal? To be better than her? Once he made it there, meaning, having impressed her, diving as well as she did, having gone as far, she left. What does that feel like? Like none of it was worth it? It being the closeness, the willingness to stay even when you're not as good, not as impressive? I get the idea to offer myself, knowing that it matters, here, that I'm a young woman, wanting to learn from him, an old—how old? A mystery-age, his face having been morphed by the sun and the risk into a wide swath of sliding scale—man. A man.

"Will you teach me to stay under that long?"

On Captain's face: a crack in solid ice. He nods, gets quiet. Then, "Anything is gonna be better than what you pulled today!"

The boat rocks its way through the water. Captain and Zeke don't know I have a dead mom. After she died, I waited a few days to tell anyone—even Tasia. The news sat with me in my quiet house. It was the hottest month on record for Berkeley and Erin refused to use the AC. I asked her if we could shut the power off too. We didn't have to change the world yet, to strip people of their understanding of Blake. Tasia would think about Blake in the present tense. An alive Blake would continue in other people's thoughts. No one would pity me and I'd still be Lydia with two moms. Somehow, I trust Michael to hold my secret, to keep Blake alive here. I move closer to Zeke and knock his arm with my fist, my teeth chattering. He knocks me back, grinning.

When we get back, Zeke and I are smiling like fools. We smell bad, sweaty and salty. Michael sits at the table wearing glasses and drinking tea. His hair is dry. He is a different species from us today, another creature entirely. Michael wants to know how it felt. The water. Being in the water. When he asks that question, "How did it feel?" I have to hold everything in my blood not to blush. When we kissed, there was the rough tangle of his beard. His lips were chapped and I wanted to run my tongue over the shape of them. Michael waits for my answer. If I do blush, I'll blame it on the cold.

"How did it feel?"

Zeke says: "I want to go diving with Captain sometime." Taking my idea. Like he wants to learn, grow, sink. I look for a reaction in Captain's face. He smirks. There's no use in saying I want to learn, too, now, because it would sound like copying. The first one to speak out loud wins? I should have said it first. I keep too much inside.

Michael turns to me and none of it matters. My loyalty to my new training, the offer to save Captain from his sad memories, it all goes out with Michael's gaze. Warmth hits my shoulders, my chest, and my stomach. "Cold," I say.

A flash of the black and gray masses in the water, the ocean filled with sea lions. As I made my way to the boat, my foot kicked rubber, the side of a sea lion, its body sloping downward. I almost felt like I lost my balance, my foot moving too quickly in response, a suspended ricochet. Can you fall if you're already in water? I took in sea water and choked. Do sea lions ever bite? Then there were Captain's arms and his hands closing around my elbows. "Worst thing they'll do is take a little nibble on your neck," he told me.

"I think," Michael says. "We have an opportunity with these missing sharks." The idea seems to show up in Michael's face, opening up his smile, filling out his cheekbones. Captain is unmoving. Before Zeke can ask him a million questions, Michael tells us we'll hear more soon. "Just hold tight," he says. I hold onto my body and hold it tight.

I know where we're going from the sounds that grow louder and surer: a hooting like monkeys, short and high-pitched sounds, as if tuning a horn; throat clearing, a guttural engine; sneezing and gurgling. Sea lions bark. Elephant seals just release, strange sounds floating and squeezing out of them like the inside of someone's stomach.

Zeke walks alongside me and my hip bumps his—an even hit, because he's nearly my height, even though he's skinnier than me, a tall blade of grass. Spooked, he skips a few steps up the path and moves faster, maintaining a pace that will keep our distance. Michael and Captain are ten or twenty feet past him, talking in hushed voices as they walk, their heads leaned in, making a triangle of the negative space between them.

The island's patchy grass gives out and the concrete path ends. We step off and onto rocks, precarious open land. To our left is a small peninsula that cuts off Mirounga Beach, a beach with a small layer of sand, where elephant seals are packed shoulder to shoulder. Further ahead and past the peninsula, the island's surface goes planetary. Sand Flat, the other place for elephant seal colonies here, is entirely missing sand. It's a large, wide, and flat area of thickly packed mud. All available surface, save for a passageway close to the peninsula wall, is filled with elephant seal bodies—large and wriggling, varying shades of yellowy brown, making up their own huge mass. Some of the animals sleep against each other, heads resting with noses hanging over the sides of the creature next to them, their breathing deep and slow. Others stack themselves on rocks closer to the water, a second story of sorts, where they groan at nesting seabirds nearby. When Michael shouts over the seals to make himself heard, I want to stick my fingers in his beard. New and tangled, mustache creeping over his top lip.

"Welcome to seal watch," he yells.

I stand with Zeke and Captain on each side of me, my team, my feet awkwardly wedged between rocks. The cliff is sharp and sudden by our feet. The elephant seals are strong and fatty, the noise they make out of a clown car. Michael explains that the primary food source for white sharks in the Farallons is elephant seals. We know the orca attack will impact the entire ecosystem here, but we don't know how. Building on an existing body of research that has tagged and tracked this elephant seal colony, we'll observe as these seals begin pupping season without their top predator.

"I want you to record the number of elephant seals on the beach every fifteen to twenty minutes," Michael explains. "And record how many individuals are entering and exiting the water." If the sharks were around, his thinking is, we'd see more elephant seals on the shore. Now that they're gone, maybe there will be an increase in the number of seals in the water, hunting, looking for food. He tells us we're scanning for pups too, but it's early for pupping—November.

We're supposed to break the third week of November for Thanksgiving. Tasia and Eugene planned to stop by the house and drop off the lemon curd that Eugene makes every year. It's too sour, Erin always tried to politely decline, but Blake liked it. I hate the idea of seeing them, of the gross wannabe jam, of Eugene's condolences face, his hand going to his waist, his hip popped as he asks me how I am. He fishes for information, then doesn't know what to do with it. He tries to care for me and then takes several steps back.

The pupping season for elephant seals on the islands starts in late December and goes through February. Captain tells us that on special years the first pups are born on Christmas Day. That's how holidays operate here, removed from the workings of the outside world, concerned with different celebrations and milestones.

Michael's shirt is not buttoned correctly. The right edge juts out past the left. Can I see his stomach, underneath his shirt, the soft skin below his belly button?

"Is shark watch over?"

"No," Michael tells me. "It's just splitting. We'll always have one man at the lighthouse, and if there's an attack, we'll boat out to it. Captain will start at the lighthouse. And you two—" I feel his attention on me, finally. "You're with me."

A place, with Michael, in continuing research here. A place!

Captain isn't sure about this plan. He didn't want to trek up to the lighthouse himself because his knee was acting up. He'd rather be on the boat, back in the water. He listens to Michael, though, even with his doubts, even with the growing sense of distrust I feel flowing from him to Michael, which Michael resists and argues against. Michael hands Captain a pair of binoculars and me another, which he instructs me to share with Zeke.

"I'll be right up there," Captain tells me, me and not Zeke, repeating what I already know is happening.

He then turns and begins the double-backed trail up to the lighthouse while Zeke and I find a good spot in the rocks. Michael should come with us but doesn't. He goes the opposite direction. I hear a high-pitched shriek I can't place as orca or bird. Captain gets smaller as he trudges up the hill. The lighthouse is short, abbreviated— two stories where it should be five or six. The hill is so much more dramatic than the structure on top of it.

We spend the day counting and taking notes as we watch the elephant seals. I slowly move the binoculars down the seals' bodies, catching on a flash of white within a pair of flippers. There—a tag. We're also supposed to jot down any tag numbers as we see them, to build a record of the individual known elephant seals that are starting their pupping season here again. As it turns out, seal watch is not as fun as shark watch. Seals mostly sleep, though sometimes they fight over territory. Different alpha males rule over colonies tucked into the rocks across the islands, most of which have been tagged and named. Not one is named Squidward, a wild mistake.

Shark watch kept me close to Michael on our small boat. Here we are stretched across the rocks. After the hours pass and the bright white clouds fade to gray and the wind picks up and the tide rises, Michael approaches.

"Can I check your notes?"

Zeke steps up with his before I can. Michael takes them and scans them, quickly, then hands them back. "Good," he says, which clearly isn't enough for Zeke, who stands there a full second before thanking Michael and stepping back. My notes are out—Michael steps closer and curves around me, reading over my shoulder instead of doing the normal human move and taking the notes into his own hands. My entire body tenses up as I try to anticipate the language we'll use with each other. Is his hand going to my shoulder? The flat private part of my lower back?

He doesn't touch me. He hovers until he stops. "Great. You can also—for fun—describe any distinct physical features you see, especially in mating individuals—alpha males and females in their harem."

"Any features?"

"You can put it in your own words," he tells me. "It doesn't have to be so formal. Be as descriptive as possible."

I'm glad he's being warm to me again, encouraging me to reroute back to myself. What I hear, in what he says to me, is that I can be good at this job by being myself. What he doesn't know, or maybe does, is how impossible that is to gauge. If I started by speaking the way guys I know speak, would that mean I was being myself? If it felt better than I'd ever felt, and I could communicate in ways that I never did, if I felt safer and surer, would it be mine? Michael sees something in me and I want to hold the image for myself. Michael sees himself in me and I hope to feel it to be true, taking on his sun-burns, his short blonde hair, his square jaw and sandy beard, his torso a big solid square. My waist dips in from the hips. I will it to widen, to strengthen, to gain muscle and mass.

The three of us walk back together in a clump, following the shaky circle of Michael's flashlight. Michael is happier, joyous, even, moving with a lightness that I haven't seen since earlier in the trip. There's Julian's athleticism in the lean muscles of his arms, in the flattening of his palms against the ground in a forward fold. I want this version of him to stretch into every day, to gather enough energy it's impossible to stop. I want it so badly that I sit in the living room tonight, not the kitchen, putting down a role I picked up when I first got here. To not cook feels like a massive and potentially dumb experiment—I'm not entirely sure that we'll eat dinner tonight—but I do it anyway, pulling out an ancient pack of Uno cards from the living room and challenging Zeke to a game.

Does Uno require any skill? Is it only luck? I don't know. We play, intensely. Zeke gets competitive very quickly. At one point he slaps the cards, even though Uno requires no slapping, and the edge of his nail goes right into my knuckle. Leaving a neat staple mark of red.

"Sorry dude," he says, yanking himself back, moving his fingers methodically through his system, touching each fingertip to his thumb.

"You're fine."

It suddenly smells like fish and olive oil, fatty and intense. A pan at the stove pops, fizzes, and hisses. Michael cooks! He shakes the pan, the fish wiggles, one hand on the handle, his chest turned away from the jumping oil. I don't know where this fish came from—it must have been stolen from the bait fridge and defrosted, which means that Michael planned ahead for this dinner. I picture him sticking his hands into the freezer and getting a fingertip stuck on a blue icepack, the skin catching, cursing quietly, freeing his finger, and continuing. Maybe he sucked on it, bringing his hand to where his body is warm and soft.

Captain comes home grumpy, but his mood lightens when he smells the fish. We eat like we haven't eaten in months, fast, messy, hungry. Oil on my chin, staining my sweatshirt, greasing my hands. Captain reports no shark sightings from the lighthouse.

"Did you see anything else up there?" I ask him. "Any whales?"

"No hon," he says. "Not today. It's not their season." He rubs his bad knee, pushing through the fabric of his jeans.

I don't hear the wind. The kitchen is warm, everyone is laughing, and I feel alive, an alive that is better than adrenaline, running on some other track in me, where the gravel is soft and the grass green and the races slow and relaxing.

Michael and Captain are still talking when Zeke and I go upstairs to bed. We keep chatting as we change in the same room at the same time. I wiggle my sports bra out of my sleeve and then take off my shirt before putting on the shitty tee I've been using as my sleep layer. My skin prickles with goosebumps. I steal a glimpse at his chest and see stretch marks along the biceps where new muscles have formed, the skin within the stretches slightly lighter and gleaming. He doesn't look at me. I layer up, then turn the lights off and climb carefully into my bed.

Zeke tells me about growing up in Eugene, where he went on camp-ing trips with his parents and two sisters in the Cascades, a mountain range that runs all the way from Canada down to the edges of the Bay Area. He often searched for salamanders with his little sisters. That detail about him never made sense to me. I can't picture him taking care of girls.

"I'm six years older than my middle sister and eight years older than the little one, so I was really in charge of them a lot. Sometimes I was more like a big cousin or uncle to them, and I don't remember what my parents were doing, but they were back at the campsite, probably, cooking or taking down our tents, while we were in the woods, looking for this rare salamander that I'd read about for like, months."

I adjust myself in bed and the entire structure creaks. Zeke, who I imagined him to be at home, stretches and morphs, he gains respon-sibility and respect.

They searched for hours, Zeke says, or what felt like it, until he heard his littlest sister scream. He ran to her, nearly eating shit on his way, and when he found her, she was holding a Larch Mountain salamander in her fist. All the air rushed into his throat and he held his breath. Before he could take the salamander from her, it bit her, drawing blood from her thumb.

"She was scared, so she threw it, and the salamander went down hard, dude, like slammed against the tree trunk. My sister's bleeding, and the salamander is twitching, and I go for the salamander."

"How old was she?"

"Four."

"Was she okay?"

"She was fine—I called Poison Control, it wasn't poisonous, but I was so mad at her. It took me a week to realize, fuck, I cared more about the animal than my own sister."

So, Zeke realized he cared about animals and the environment by choosing them over his own family. That's his origin story to this work, to marine biology, learning via his own impulse, from what corner of the living space demanded his attention. Yes, sort of, he allows, but it wasn't that direct or fast—in fact, he avoided this line of work for a long time because he felt guilty he didn't care more about other people.

"I don't see it that way," I tell him. "That you didn't care. You just knew who needed your help the most and it was the salamander."

"Maybe," Zeke says. "You know hella salamanders are lungless?"

"Literally?"

"Yeah, they breathe through their skin."

I like Zeke more now than I have ever liked him. I try to fall asleep, even though I have a friend now. When I turn onto my side, I feel my phone through the mattress, a tiny elbow into my right thigh.

Seal watch continues. The numbers slowly grow as we creep deeper into November. Even though there are rare sunny days, the wind is intense, and the boat with our supplies gets delayed and delayed. When I watch Michael with his clipboard, I wonder if he's ever thinking about the woman who first introduced him to elephant seals. At the end of one cold day, where Zeke and I shiver so much our data sheets become chicken scratch, Michael gives me a sidehug, bringing me under his arm and shoulder. He's not much taller than me, so

I bend to accept it, my spine curling, which tilts my head into his chest. Once I'm there, he shakes me, lightly, squeezing and swaying me. "Gotta get you warm again." I'm suddenly in middle school again.

The kiss is building in my mind, stretching and growing, taking more room, stealing the space usually given to other thoughts, but it's not asking for anything, rather than dreaming into the next move, my brain is slowing, and the kiss is starting to simmer as proof instead of prediction, proof that Michael cares about me, that I'm a whole adult, that I am seen and respected.

The sand at the elephant seal colony by North Landing is eroding, making the seals haul up on the rocks, sometimes displacing birds or crushing nests. Murres, one of the many birds here, make nests that are not so much structures but spots, specific cracks in the rock that a bird chooses and comes back to year after year. They're monogamous and they mate for life. I could remember the same slice of rock for my lifetime, especially if it was a shared memory with someone who loved me. I shove my feet under the rocks, their heaviness a comfort, my toes squished into my soles.

Sometimes I roast Zeke for his notes, his attempts at describing physical seal features with specificity. I let him know he's not being funny, just mean, when he tries to roast mine. We compete for Best Notes, an award we decide based on the feedback Michael gives us. I will always think that I won.

The water stays turquoise in the shallowest parts even when it's cold and gray out. It's not a color drawn out by the sun, it just is. Whenever I start to feel good, a real good, good that continues, that roots in all corners of me, good that I get so attached to, there's terror too. I want to kill the terror, push it away, but the two are married, attached, the edge of happiness blowtorch sealed to fear's tail, and if I have one, I've got to put up with the other.

There is one disgusting day where Michael doesn't show up and I can't find him at the lighthouse and Captain dodges all questions about where or how he is and a seagull poops on me and Zeke can't get it out of my hair. There are more elephant seals, a new bull, who challenges #48, Mr. De Niro, for his title. When he body rolls close, De Niro lifts his head up, looking about a thousand pounds, a crease folds a third down his fatty nose, the wrinkles so dense it resembles a face full of coral, sharp and pink, and he opens his mouth, wide. His nose nearly falls into his throat, but he's still able to make a sound, a loud, nasally clicking, a foghorn mixed with a grandfather clock. The new bull winces, turns, gets lost. I write it all down and still Michael doesn't show.

Zeke wants to compare notes anyway but I'm not in the mood. The numbers of elephant seals on land seemed to dip, supporting Michael's hypothesis, but have now spiked again, maybe because breeding happens on land? Captain, who sees my moods, suggests that he take us somewhere new at the end of our day.

"I don't want to swim," I say, "No offense."

Captain leads us along until he pauses and climbs over the concrete path's edge, a gentle bumper. I stay where I'm standing, on the path. Zeke assures me it's fine. When we got here, Michael told us how important our footsteps were. He suggested we treat the path as a kid's game. The path is solid ground, the rest is hot lava that can swallow you up.

With Captain and Zeke, lava is made safe, but I catch myself watching my feet anyway. Captain takes us to a gathering of wooden boxes, scattered across the hillside. They resemble very sturdy shoe boxes, ones that have been kept and collected outside—the top lids held down by rocks. Captain tells us that birds are kept here during nesting season. They sit on their eggs and keep them warm here. Every few days, every week, researchers come out, lift the rock that holds the box closed, and check to see how the bird is doing.

Sometimes birds don't mate and don't nest, and sometimes researchers have no idea why. Do the birds being pulled out of boxes want to be touched? Their wings are spread, gently, measured and compared to other birds, to records of other years where birds were bigger or smaller. Then there's the dark again, relief, the small sound of the rock being replaced on the top of the box, the bird's body heat back, building, and focused entirely on the egg underneath them.

"I've watched this place for a very long time," Captain keeps talking, his frame a large shadow tilting over the view. "I've cared for it." I'm barely listening, suddenly flooded with intense gratitude, because here holidays are not holidays, they don't have to mean what they mean to my family.

Erin planned to have a tree this year and I said it would be stupid. Will the house smell like pine needles when I get back? Maybe she'll have gotten rid of the tree and the effort to pretend things are normal. That's not even right, because it's impossible to pretend things are normal, without Blake. Getting a tree is going ahead with the traditions we used to have and hoping they will still hold meaning. Erin once sculpted a Nativity scene out of clay and now insists on displaying it every year, Jesus the size and shape of a jellybean.

Zeke asks Captain what his favorite job here has been. Captain laughs, and it's a different laugh than I've heard before, more brittle, like it could snap in half. He has done every sort of job there is here: led white shark tours on tourist boats around the islands, dived his dangerous dives for sea urchins, selling them to seafood markets in Chinatown and upscale sushi restaurants, sought out lost boats and precious metals for bootleg marine salvage operations, driven the boat for researchers, cleaned the house for researchers, harpooned sharks for researchers, run equipment rooms for researchers. Once he was working for researchers, he was on the island, his two feet on this land, no longer encircling it.

"Is it better to be on the water or on the rocks?" I ask.

He doesn't laugh at this question. He's not sure. "The early entrepreneurs of the island obviously thought, rocks. Do you know the history of eggers here?" Zeke nods yes and I shake my head no. He doesn't care that Zeke will be bored by what follows. "1850s San Francisco had run out of chicken eggs. Eggers discovered that the California murre produced a very similar egg—most seabirds make eggs that are slimy and fishy. They egged until they piled mountains of egg several men high." He reaches out to squeeze my arm. "I'll show you the pictures. Decimated the murre population."

Captain thinks that he could have sensed the tipping point, the moment where egging had gone too far, claimed so many eggs from the murres that bird populations would not recover for years. The eggers needed someone with his sight and hearing, with his sensibility, just as Michael needed him now. Maybe Captain wants to be Michael, not just Michael's body parts. When Michael is missing, Captain's a good leader—does he want credit for that? Would he rather lead more? Does he desire to start expeditions, make the choices that take us from sharks to seals? Captain is wise, kind, capable, but when he speaks at length about anything, his tone starts to grieve whatever the subject is.

"Where's Michael?" I ask again.

"I'm sorry," he says. "He's better when he's not drinking."

Not drinking. A distant alarm sounds in my head but I silence it quickly. My nose is numb by the end of the tour. On our return to the house, Zeke hangs back a few steps. Captain keeps walking.

"Is Michael an alcoholic?"

Zeke's surprised. The question popped into my head before I got too scared to ask it, my body descending into a deep, anticipatory calm.

"Yeah, he's sober," he says. He thought I already knew that. I tell him I didn't. I ask him if he likes working for Michael. He says yeah, that Michael can be a loose cannon but he knows everything about this place. A loose cannon, another thing I haven't seen Michael be. I skip past that, ask Zeke about Michael's ex-wife, if he's ever met her, letting my brain and mouth go automatic, free association. Sometimes I've thought about her, Julian's mom, and she is a blank face in my head asking for features.

"She was nice," Zeke tells me, peering at me strangely but answering anyway. He met her once when Michael got too drunk at the Japanese restaurant in the marina. Zeke had tried to keep up with

Michael and Captain, and was also very drunk, so he planned to abandon his car in the parking lot and come back for it later in the day. It was a Sunday afternoon and Michael's wife had been on a bike ride.

When she showed up, she was sweaty, wearing a highlighter yellow windbreaker. Her bike was attached to the top of her Subaru. Michael's limbs were elastic and it was hard to get him into the car. His wife thanked Zeke but did not offer him a ride home. She left quickly. The parking lot was very sunny and Captain had disappeared. So, Zeke took a nap in the grass by where kids fly kites on a windy day; when he woke up it was dark, and he felt more sober, and drove home.

I don't know why I want to know more about Michael's wife in place of Michael. I'm not interested in how long he's been sober, or what kind of sober he is, instead, there's the even oval where her face is supposed to be. "One of my moms was an addict," I imagine telling Zeke. And he says: "Moms? Was?"

I ask him what she looked like, and he just says she looked like a Berkeley mom. I tell Zeke that Michael's son got sick, and he wanted me to take care of him and instead I took his place on this trip as a substitute. "He didn't break up with me. I left. I don't know why I lied to you about it but I did," I say.

"It's all good," he says, his words picking up speed, the edges of his mouth slippery triangles, "We're here now, aren't we?" And out of his pocket comes the rounded shape of a whiskey bottle. I try to whisper when I ask him where he got it. He laughs and says he brought it with him, of course. He's older and can buy alcohol without scheming. As I slow my step, a mouse darts over my toes thick in their boots and I jump but don't scream. The mouse, brown-ish and whiskered, is the smallest creature I've seen on the island, save for the bugs. I hold the image of Michael, sitting at the kitchen table, dirty or clean, the sound of the opening door tipping his eyeline to me and the rest of the group walking in.

But when we get back to the house, Michael is nowhere to be found. The kitchen table is empty and the room cold. I'm concerned. My chest heavy, I wash my hands in the sink and ask Zeke for help with dinner. He opens and drains cans of beans and corn, while I dice peppers and onions. The corners of my eyes leak. In another bowl I pour cornbread mix in with vegetable oil and honey. The honey is a trick from Erin, who likes fancying up the not-fancy.

After dinner, Zeke and I put whiskey into hot cups of black tea. I listen for Michael. It starts to rain. The outside of the house grows colder and the sound of rain hitting the reinforced metal roof gets louder. Water grows spikes out here, develops hard edges. I'd forgotten this new sensation, how excited alcohol makes me, lighting up the edge of a flammable inside. An old version of my mom flickers and fades—her laughing loudly, her dancing until sweat plastered her hair to the sides of her neck. Are the feelings that I have when I'm drunk hers? Does whiskey make me bigger and stronger? Does it make me more dangerous? Do I make terrible choices? What do bad decisions feel like?

Besides his tantrum, Zeke has softened over the course of our time here. He's my friend and can't avoid it. He's definitely not trying to hit on me, which feels good. That's not the type of attention I want from him, and it can be nice to be safe from that way of being seen entirely. We have lived in the same house, sharing a bunk bed, and tonight, drunk, he becomes my big brother. He sucked at it before, but he might be better now—I don't mind it. Maybe my moms could've had another kid. They ran out of my donor's donation at some point. It was hard to get pregnant. If they wanted another kid with the same guy, they would have needed to ask him to come back.

The bottle of whisky goes empty and I am drunk, drunk in this strange place where there is nothing but us and this house. Zeke and I laugh, too loudly. Then there is a sound, a sound that can only be categorized as the sound of a door, first opening, then closing. But I can see the front door and it's unmoving.

"What?" I say to Zeke.

He looks at me blankly. "There's a back door." My heart races. Michael. He's back. Zeke's face starts to slide and he says we should go to bed. I quickly agree. We're suddenly tiptoeing in the way that you can only do when you're fucked up. Dramatic and imaginary-quiet, like holding your breath before dropping something precious and it breaking into a million pieces on the floor. Zeke nearly loses his balance and lurches his hand into my shoulder for emergency support. My cheeks tighten holding in laughter. Zeke goes up the stairs and everything inside me gets me to stop. I tell him two people on the stairs will be too loud, and also, I need some water. He nods, salutes me, and takes the stairs very slowly, with one hand on each railing, as if pulling himself to the top. I sneak back to the sink, where I fill up a cup with water, waiting.

There's a front door and backdoor but only one staircase. The sound of footsteps gets me to drop to the ground. I don't want Michael to see me. I'm under the kitchen table and there's water at my feet. I spilled. A light clicking hits the air and I'm in darkness—he must have turned off the lights. I peer around the table legs to search for him in the dark, locating only a fuzzy shadow that climbs the stairs, like Zeke did, disappearing upstairs. I will find him, I will find him. I crawl on all-fours to the stairs, bumping my knee hard against the table or some other solid obstacle. I limp up and I make it to the second floor. I trace the wall with my fingers until I find his door and I stand there.

My hand pushes his door open and I slide into Michael's room and make a noise to tell him I'm there. My eyes adjust to let in the dark room—his bed with rumpled comforter, his desk with papers and lamp, a pair of jeans thrown over the top of a rolling chair. The room is small. It smells of wood and dust. There's the shine of Michael's eyes as he sees me and moves his torso up and out of the covers. I keep my eyes connected to him even though it's terrifying and I wait, wait for him to do anything, to speak, for the window to open so I can climb inside.

When cats trust you, they close their eyes around you—they take long, sleepy blinks, as if they are demonstrating the open-shut of their eyelids. I want to trust this room and this man, so I blink slow, and my eyes shut, and the feeling is cozy, my inside dark, letting what's tired sit down, my dark matches the room, I am blinking, but to blink you have to open your eyes—

When I'm standing over the bed, his arms are open. I move into them. The sheets on this side of the bed are cool and his skin is warm. The bed is smaller than I expected. My cheek rubs against his chest, maybe, it's smooth, sweaty. I'm sweaty. My clothes are peeled off and I breathe black tea whiskey into that chest, which dips like a slight crater in the middle, then lips, my sweat sticking and pulling against his, I don't know what I feel. His mustache scrapes against my cheeks. Up close he smells like skin. Salt and dew soured by breath. Laundry detergent and dirt, the soap far away. My body is loud and beating, and it responds to his hands, and the sheets get warm, and I can't figure out if I stepped in or I was pulled.

The bed is too small, I almost fall. I'm aware, suddenly, of the axes of my body, on a plane far away from the ground, too close to him. Underneath me and around me, there is me, but there's a separation, like my movements are several steps delayed behind my thoughts. He finally speaks but I don't like the sound of his voice, and I tell him to be quiet. Shhh, I'm clamoring for him but everything is messy, I can barely trace where I am and what is happening. There is a body in front of me and a hand reaching down my pants. My hips meet bone, my hands meet dick that is fumbling out of his pants, none of this is smooth.

The dark is swallowing. I'm drunk, two steps behind, my own shadow trying to keep up with me. The idea of him fills me so wholly that I can't trust whether or not we are really touching. Am I dreaming, some vivid dream of the room I have imagined with all its objects inside? I've thought about his abandoned clothes at the end of the day. Where he puts his dirty shirts. If he throws his jeans over a chair or dresser after he peels them off. A sock stuck to old carpeting. I try to hold on. His skin, rougher than mine, the sweat making it catch and fold over itself. My mouth is dry, giving him everything, I am so thirsty, I'd like an orange soda.

Julian's body felt new. His skin tight across the muscles of his chest, abs that made themselves when he tensed up, neat fingernails and smooth skin. He walked through the world with an ease, and he was good with his hands, but when he fucked, he became geometric, a hinge that swung open and closed. Everything that was mysterious about him disappeared, and he was the kind of machine that makes the same product over and over again. He was inside me but I did not feel that I was with him. Michael is different. Here in his bed he becomes elastic. His tongue presses against the round of my belly button as he shows me what he would do if he were lower. I think he asks if he can keep going and I say yes.

We've experienced things together. That I know. Did I run onto the rocks or dip deeper into the water where I find my food? Have the sharks left? Am I where it's safe? Am I where it feels good?

I wake up in my own bed. The thick blanket is tucked into the end like at a hotel, squeezing my toes into the sheets. The sides of my head feel caved in. I am achy and hungover. My face is wet with drool and my neck is sweaty and so are my squished feet. I wake up with the jolt of adrenaline that comes after I drink, thinking that I've missed something or that there is something I must go fix, and fast. When I woke up with stitches after fucking up my arm, the adrenaline and dread were still there, even though my body had already been literally fixed. Immediately I wonder if I should be embarrassed.

The fog has since captured the whole island, multiplied and spread, so heavy it's as if the clouds have lowered themselves to person level. The path disappears into a line that stops. The house's windows forced into gray squares, the color with no depth. Everything outside us just ends. Thanksgiving trip home is a no-go. More food is a no-go. Erin wanted to hear how I was doing on the satellite phone and I told her I had to get back to work.

I don't remember how last night ended, and I don't remember how I got here. Michael must have brought me here. Did Zeke hear him? Seeing me in his arms, did Zeke think I had passed out? I guess I did pass out. Or fell asleep. I am disoriented trying to find the last thing I felt. Tasia's postcard on the wall stares at me, a Swedish postcard of a beautiful boy-girl skier in underwear, holding two skis criss-cross across their chest, feet in sneakers pushing into the snow. Their face is tilted up into the sun, and their eyes are closed. Their sky is blue and bright. It's the one detail of this room that I'm responsible for, except my dirty clothes in the corner.

When I put weight on the wooden rungs of the bunkbed ladder, there's sweat on my heel that slides me forward. A small pain, a slicing. I clatter to the ground, where I lift my foot to my palm to see the wood splinter that has lodged itself into me. Zeke groans and turns away, still asleep, his face to the wall, the blankets shoved over his head. I sleep in a goddamn bunk bed. How was I tucked in? With an audience? With my weight in my toes, I limp to the bathroom and run the water. Today it's my special gift to take a three-minute hot shower and I've never been more grateful for anything in my entire life. I forgot what hot water felt like.

I sit down in the shower, meeting the ground, a small square of gray. In order to fit, my thighs squeeze up against the wall and the glass door. I put my legs into some sort of yoga twist so I can see the splinter. I tug down the bar of soap and make it into suds before I wash my foot and everything around the splinter. The heat and soapy water will flood it out. The suds rinse away and there is my foot, bright red from the heat of the water, still splintered. My fingernails try to pinch it away but the top just snaps off into a fingertip. Then it is the smallest freckle, an imperfect dot, staring at me.

Every summer Tasia asked me, "Do I have freckles yet?" Last time there was a dot on her upper lip that could have been a blackhead or a new freckle. I tried to squeeze it out for her, then admitted defeat.

I give up. I shampoo and condition my hair sitting down, quickly, rushing, the hot water running itself in circles around my neck. By the time I'm rinsing the conditioner out the water is cold. I close my eyes and try to pretend it's the ocean, and it gets so frigid I almost believe it.

In the glass door's reflection, a rare mirror, my face is mine and not: red-cheeked and baggy-eyed, slick, asleep, clean, awake, dirty, young, old. I thought I had my own face until I started listening to what my moms told me. They were right. In Erin's baby photos, there was my face on hers.

Is Michael awake and looking at himself? His face probably looks different from mine, not hungover, more slept. I try on his thoughts, but they slip away from me. Maybe he's waking up from his creaky bed and shaking his head, he can't believe himself. He thinks back to the moment we kissed, watching the orcas kill the shark, and wonders if that's where whatever this is started, or if he felt attraction before then and noted it to himself, like a warning or blessing, a closeness he wanted to happen but thought shouldn't, or wanted to happen but thought wouldn't. He wakes up as if it did, and the face he finds is not his either: fucked up, made anew, his wrinkles a reminder, proud and shamed but not so ashamed that he couldn't sleep.

I feel sick, a deeper sick than the hangover, a dread that tells me I fucked up. He's not in his usual spot downstairs. I wanted him to respect me enough to sleep with me. The kitchen table is empty. I wanted him to respect me enough not to sleep with me. In the living room, there he is, his body crooked in one of the house's mismatched thrift store armchairs. Him in the light. Now that Michael exists in front of me and not just in my head, I search him for guilt, excitement, regret, pride. I try to relax my shoulders. What is a normal stance? Should I slouch? Find a wall to lean against?

Michael says: "Fog rolled in."

"Yeah. Visibility okay?"

Michael grimaces. "No." He's not how I pictured him. There's a pink to the white of his eyes, extra lines underneath them, his skin puffy. As bad as me. His cheeks are bare. They look soft. No beard. No beard? He shaved when he woke up this morning and he looks more like Julian now. It's disconcerting.

"Sleep okay?"

"Yes."

"When are we off?"

"You're on shark watch today with Captain. Zeke's with me."

"Okay," I manage. And then, before I can hold it inside, "Why today, though?" The accusation spits out of me. I've been on seals since we started the new project. Michael asks if we're clear. He tells me there are dishes in the sink. I just nod.

When I slip back into our room, Zeke sits up in the bottom bunk, wiping the crust from his eyes. He's grumpy and grumbling, telling me to pick up my shit from the corner, and yeah, he heard me almost eat shit this morning. Did Michael see the dirty clothes in the corner?

"Why did you leave so early?" He groans. "It would have been funny if it wasn't so fucking loud." I gather my clothes in my arms and sit in the corner, looking out through the cloudy glass. He pokes his head out from his bunk, "Last night was fun."

He looks bad too, hair greasy and smeared across his forehead, mustache so long it's nearly growing into his mouth, eyes red and bleary. His shirt is off. His arms seem long and impossibly gangly, the fingertips stretching like the end of a hand wearing too-long plastic gloves. I don't know what he saw or heard, if he saw me last night, after we said goodnight, in Michael's arms or drunkenly stumbling in, if he saw me undress, if he caught me stumble as I tried to get up into the top bunk. His chest is basically hairless. It holds a small space in the middle, a gap between the pecs.

"Yeah," I tell Zeke, in a daze. I can smell the alcohol on him. I keep my eyes fixed outside. "Can you leave so I can get dressed, please."

He laughs before realizing I'm serious. "Okay, old school. That's fine." He gets ready and I remain there, stay until I grab the binoculars from the equipment room, and out those cloudy glass windows, I see Zeke join Michael outside, their figures tiny in the distance.

Captain meets me outside. It's foggy, and cold. Fall disintegrating into winter, slowly freezing. Wind whips around the island, gaining speed around the corners. The lighthouse looms over us, its hill separating our side of the island from the other. When we work from Mirounga Beach, the beach that holds one of the elephant seal colonies, I can see Captain or Zeke at the lighthouse, made into a stick figure. When we make it to our vantage point today, I should be able to see Zeke and Michael from above. Maybe I'll survey them, instead of the waters, for shark attacks.

Captain sees my state, my attitude, my sweat, the curled-up expression on my face. Whatever went wrong last night seeps through my pores, and he can smell it, so he moves slowly. He has a bad knee, so there's the possibility he's not making any adjustments for me, but as we hit the steep incline of lighthouse hill and make our first switchback, he takes an exaggerated deep breath, squeezing the railing, even stopping to reapply sunscreen to his nose in one large white clump, I believe his behavior is directed toward me.

The hill is even steeper than it looks, and that's partially because the ground isn't solid—it's rocky, dusty, crumbly, the surface layer constantly shedding and ditching its pieces. Old bird boxes are scattered between rocks, the wood wet and dark. The lighthouse base widens as we get closer. The concrete is growing moss, maybe even barnacles. The sun is hidden behind the fog, too obstructed to feel it warming us. I float backward when I don't squeeze my abs in, gravity and the wind peeling me away from the trail and into the wide expanse of island below. It feels more right to fall here than it does to stay on trail, another moment where the island communicates directly to us that we are weak, small, and unwanted. I am weak, small, unwanted.

Dread ripples around my belly button. What I'm doing is dangerous. I could slip and fall, I could throw up and pass out. The stakes of my body today are high and I wish that my needs didn't read so clearly and directly on my face.

"One more switchback," Captain says. I'd stopped, hung my head over my feet, and the ground was starting to sway with my breathing.

"I can't do it," I tell him. And I really can't. My legs have given up and I can't get any air into my lungs. It's not a good place to stop. The incline is really steep and the nearest portion of railing bitten away and rotting, but I give in to my need, and then there's no other choice. I sit down, wrapping my right arm around the leg of the railing, clinging to its damp wood. How am I going to get myself out of this? To turn around and go back down means using my knees, controlling my body, staying low and together. To make it to the lighthouse means finding power I don't have, burning energy that's already gone. What does it mean to give up?

I fumble around to put my hand on my chest, to feel my heart rate so I can regulate my breathing, and all I find is the flat bone of my sternum, a plate underneath the skin. Zeke's chest is not so flat. It dips. Michael's chest—last night's chest—a similar crater. Are all men's chests built like that? The skin was so smooth. I feel sick. Captain's knee pushes into the gravel next to me. He kneels and the posture probably hurts. He claps his hands.

"That's enough," he says.

"I can't," I repeat.

He takes his sunglasses off, squinting, revealing the pillowy bags under his eyes, so substantial they're fluffy, like they'd squish if you put your fingers to them. "Good science means you gotta be there," he says. "That's it. You gotta be there for the long and the short, even if you've got a mean hangover." He points to the top of the trail, the looming lighthouse, the sun behind clouds. "We're fuckin' close, Lydia. I know you have it."

When I was little, Blake took me to visit her father in San Francisco a handful of times, not enough to become recurring visits, because they ultimately stopped, and I sometimes felt this way with him, like he had summoned up all his good will and coughed it out onto me, then stood there, waiting for me to metabolize the love. Blake's dad was small, his back curved. He lost an arm in Vietnam and used a claw attachment that strapped onto his stub, the skin rounding and ending not far below the shoulder. He made turkey burgers for me, securing the pan handle with his claw and flipping the patty with his hand. If he was trying to father or grandfather me, he was shouting from very far away and ex- pecting I fix my hearing. He could get Blake to laugh so hard she got incurable hiccups, and soon enough she'd be plugging her ears and drinking water upside down through a straw to get rid of them.

I pick myself up and walk the remaining leg of the trail, which gets even steeper, so steep that I bend my knees and lean in. Rock chips scatter and fall behind me. Captain doesn't say much after that but offers the occasional "Good," murmured in low and gruff tones. We make it, the trail finally, suddenly, evening out to a small flat area. The lighthouse's sides are covered with a bright, grassy green moss, the huge glass-encased light at its top thick and dull. Hanging just above the lighthouse is the blurry outline of the sun through the clouds, more illuminated now. I tilt my face toward it and unzip my jacket. Trying to let the sun in. That's what Erin's description of sobriety used to be: letting the sun in and staying there.

I never found out the reason we stopped visiting Blake's dad. She went to his funeral years later when I was in high school, alone.

Around the lighthouse is a small circle of raised concrete. We drop our bags and step onto the platform, where Captain takes out his binoculars and scans. The concrete is hard and cold against my back, supporting everything as I pant and catch my breath. We are so high the islands appear flat from here, unrolled into a wild and moving map. The fog starts to burn off, the clouds thinning, revealing all the places we've tagged sharks: the round, huge top of Sugarloaf, streaked with white bird poop, the peak across from lighthouse hill, sharper and uneven, with pointed tips, the rundown shack perched right at Mirounga Bay. Captain tells me that's an old egger's house.

He's so eager today, Captain, to jump in where I stop. Walking, looking, speaking. He's watching me closely, and I don't like that he might see weakness in me, or worse, that he sees a slutty girl, or even worse than that, a victim of something. His kindness protects me, which views me as breakable, which means that he can see a wound. I want to tell him, there is no wound! His binoculars hang at his neck, the strap turning his burnt neck white. Far below him I spot our two human shapes, Michael and Zeke, standing and sitting at different points above the elephant seals. I can't tell what they're doing. Paranoia hits, that Michael does this with every young hire, that Captain knows it, that he enables it, that he knows everything about what I've experienced with Michael. Captain and Michael talk about me at the end of the day, laughing and making inappropriate jokes. How stupid I was to think I could hold onto my privacy here.

I look past them to the water. There's a surprise burst of water and mist. I yell it, "WHALE!" and Captain swings his binoculars around and confirms, "Hooooo wee. Good eye, kid." There's that kindness again, his familiarity with me. I side-eye it. In the binoculars, I find the whale's back the next time it resurfaces, a strange and slick surface with two apple-seed shaped holes. The binoculars make possible a wild kind of sight, not just extending the scope of my vision but clarifying it too, so I feel an imposed focus when I'm looking through them, a fixed gaze that gives me all the details of what's in front of me. They make me a better listener and observer.

The wind whistles as it brushes the sides of the lighthouse. I miss the warmth of the night before, the gravel of Michael's skin, the pull that brought me so close I thought my body could collapse into his like an amoeba. A place for my fist, a whole hand, in the crater of his chest. The hangover is fading but the nausea is back. From last night, a new image—a t-shirt torso coming down onto me, ribs poking me hard in the stomach. A quick apology, either his voice for jabbing me or my voice for getting jabbed. Girls apologize for themselves, for their existence. I didn't want to be like that. When was there ever a shirt?

The torso doesn't seem like Michael, but I tell the nausea that it was—that he was what Julian couldn't be and it's all very confusing, that what I experienced, I experienced with Michael. I never understood when people described their toes curling in sex and now I do, as if someone's touch connects you so deeply to yourself that everything drops down to exist on the same line. There's no slack on the rope that runs through you, and it gets pulled as someone learns how to touch you, how to reach into the part of you that responds.

The day rolls on slowly. I keep my binoculars on the water, searching for fins and blood, but there are none. Seals in the water, yes. Northern fur seals, elephant seals, and sea lions. Are there more than usual? I can't tell, tugged away from my data sheets, my daily elephant seal counts. I want there to be some conclusion in the natural world today, some dramatic symbol of progress or change. When a white shark is killed, the surrounding sharks feel the loss right away. How long does it take for the sharks' prey to know it's safer than normal, that it isn't a fluke?

I try to eat a peanut butter sandwich but it's too dry. The stale bread adds a cast to my teeth.

It starts to get dark. The house a shadow below us. Captain is ready to call it a day. What if I don't return? I'll sleep in the lighthouse tonight, make a home out of Michael's sanctuary, stay where it's cold, wet, alone, and there's good TV. Is the lighthouse room how I saw it in my head?

"Let's go," Captain says, and I don't move.

"I bet we could see one. If we stayed."

"That's wishful thinking."

"Maybe," I say, the nausea not so much back as persisting, not leaving, my throat tightening. I'd like to see Michael, but the way he looked at me this morning, it was blank, dismissive, so lacking that it felt like an attack, an actual pushing away. His newly smooth face. Was there some stubble along his jawline? I was the sort-of girlfriend to his son and that fact sticks to me like a wet t-shirt today. How could he view me with anything but shame? I'm the embodiment of a poisonous energy for him, an unnatural occurrence, a betrayal.

Captain might actually try to touch me, rest a hand on my shoulder, he's growing so concerned, and to remain stubborn about staying would mean allowing his concern to build, to bear him trying to help me in some way. Captain tells me, "You don't want to be on this trail in the dark," and even though I know Michael does it all the time, I let that be the answer and I move. The way down is just as steep. Captain goes first, using the railing to support each step. The birds yell and the sea lions bark. The fog thickens and the sky starts to leak as we make it back to the house.

Zeke waits for me just inside the door. He tugs at my jacket, diverting me from the staircase. His cotton t-shirt is layered over a green long sleeve. Stubble speckles his chin, populates the skin below his mustache.

"I missed you today," he says. He looks younger, dumber, smiling at me all funny. "Seal watch sucks without you."

"Yeah, I feel like shit."

His too-long arms come for me, looping me into his chest. We don't touch like this. "I'm sorry," he says, "You can blame me!"

I lightly punch his chest, feeling the bones hit my knuckles, creating separation between us. "I just never want to be hungover again."

Zeke releases me, rubbing the spot I hit, no longer laughing. Shame runs through me, what he could have seen this morning, then the torso emerges again, its holey chest, its boney body colliding with me. The images I have of last night are limited. I have the beginning, and pieces of the middle, but not the end. I can't account for all of myself.

"Sometimes it's worth it," he says.

Confused, I escape to the kitchen, where I make mashed potatoes for dinner from a box with a lackluster packet of gravy. Captain opens a bottle of red wine. He pours everyone a cup, save for Michael, and the look I see Michael give Captain, a resentment that slithers, is familiar to me. This has happened before. Many times before. There's quiet, and then Michael asks, and Captain says no, and Michael's face is suddenly warm with boiling anger.

Michael doesn't seem more than Julian tonight, in fact, watching him as the muscles in his neck bulge, as he squirms in his seat, he seems less, reduced to the same age we are, the same plane. He accepts the no, but dinner is uncomfortable, and I, still queasy, hoping the gravy will absorb the alcohol from last night and this new wine, want things to be different. Why won't he act like an adult?

Erin would ask Blake: "Are you drinking?" Erin never asked: "Did you drink?" She asked the question as it related to a continuous action. Blake did not drink and stop, she either had not drunk or she was drinking. Eventually Erin stopped asking. I wondered if it was because she knew the answer to the question, or that it didn't matter to her anymore.

I leave to use the bathroom and when I come back, condensation drips down the sides of a near-empty wine bottle. Michael's lips are slightly purple, his hands wrapped around the chipped mug. He's drinking. It's a change so quick that I almost feel as if I'm making it up. Surprisingly, it hurts. No, maybe the drinking makes the impossible possible, maybe it erases the tension or allows me to ignore it. Drinking is what brought me close to Michael once and it will do so again. I should have been drinking this entire time, then

I could have shared something with him. He's going to trek out to the lighthouse for the Warriors game soon.

Zeke told me there's a single mattress, memory foam, and TV stand inside the lighthouse. Zeke—also drunk?—keeps trying to get my attention and I ignore him. Captain chastises him when he tries to refill his cup too quickly. Maybe I'll try to follow Michael, and he'll allow it or not. Captain mentions we might be able to see helicopters toward the end of our time here. Scouting for a special mission that's headed up by MARO, the same government-backed nonprofit that funds our research.

"Will a new group of researchers move in right away?" I ask, and Captain smirks. "Not exactly."

Michael, prickled, elbows Captain, "It's not set in stone yet. I've got faith, some, in the appeals process."

"MARO is way too powerful," Captain says. I sip my wine, worrying about my teeth and the potential stains. Sensing my confusion, he turns and explains that the mice here are a real problem. They're invasive and the population is growing every year. And the bird people at MARO are concerned, because the owls come in and eat the mice when they're supposed to be migrating, and because the owls are still around, they also eat ashy storm petrels, a species in danger of going extinct. Captain stops, clears his throat.

"So, the fuckin' genius solution is to drop poison pellets all over the island, which will kill the mice, but it'll also take out a whole other chunk of animals."

How do mice connect in the chain to the orcas, to the sharks? If the sharks leave, is that good for the mice? Bad? I ask what predator the owls have here, wondering if there's an orca that could save the ashy storm petrel, to jump start the owls' migration. They don't have any, that's the problem, Zeke tells me, reaching to grip my shoulder for emphasis, and when I slide away from his hand, he tells Captain he doesn't think it'll happen. They've been talking about it for years at this point. Captain is unmoved. He is right about these kinds of things. He was right many years ago when...

Michael gets up and excuses himself. I'm no longer listening to Captain. Everyone's plates are empty now, even Zeke's, and I rush to clear the table, getting the dishes to the sink, where I start to scrub. Zeke protests, "I was gonna do them tonight," his voice miles behind me. When Michael comes back, he'll slip out the door to the lighthouse and I'll follow. The window above the sink, clouded and slicked with rain, reminds me of the storm outside. I do the dishes quickly, lightly slicing myself as I dry the knife, then hustle to our room and grab my raincoat, hat, and neck warmer.

My feet nearly slip on the stairs as I round the banister into the kitchen. Michael is lacing up his shoes at the door. Zeke and Captain are still sipping their wine at the table. Captain takes my abandoned cup and dumps the remainders into his. Aware that I will be following Michael with an audience, I try to move lightly on my feet, sliding across the room until I'm close and he notices me, notices me with all my gear on.

"Can I watch the game with you?"

Michael's face goes blank, his eyes darting to the table with Zeke and Captain, then back to me, and he half nods, keeping a real answer private, or just out of my reach, and motions with his hands for me to come closer, pointing at his shoes, "Get laced up." Warmth floods me, a spring-like adrenaline in a winter storm, and my hands nearly shake as I put my shoes on, then we are outside, where the wind and cold hits with a force. My leg muscles kick in, making a concerted effort to keep me standing. I survey the gray, the lighthouse a messy flash on its peak, but Michael takes a hard left, sticking close to the perimeter of the house, his head tucked down. I follow, like this walk is our secret, already feeling included into a secrecy that is just mine and his.

He stops when we reach a side of the house without windows. Rain drops already speckle his coat, the wind pulling strands of his hair out of the hood. He squares his shoulders to me and seems to stop himself before talking. I have nerves, all of a sudden, I don't know what he's going to say but this type of privacy is threatening, then says: "Are you having a nice time here?" A nice time. He wants to know if I'm having a nice time.

"Yeah. I love it here." Love was the wrong word to use. Too big, used too casually. I pause to see if anything rushes the space. "I'm learning a lot, I guess."

"Good." He leans against the house, the side of his left arm flattening into the wood. Protecting himself from the rain, angling me toward the storm. "Are you a Warriors fan?"

"Sort of." Maybe we're sheltered here until the rain lets up. "I think they could be really good this year."

"Me too." He sighs. "But I've been a fan a long time."

Why are we here? I'm getting anxious. The rain doesn't seem to ebb and flow. We're not waiting for a natural window. He waits for something else.

"Look," he says, and the tenor of his voice changes, getting gentle, moving slower, "I realize I have made mistakes."

I like the infinite possibility of this moment, how scary it feels.

"Mistakes?"

"Yes. I recognized myself in you and that was inappropriate. I think I took things a step too far." My wrists sting. He says, "I'm not stupid." I wince. He says, "I know you have a crush. I've respected that and tried to keep my boundary as your boss. Not perfectly, I know." My fingernails curl into my palm, pressing down. "But this behavior, following me, getting me alone, it has to stop. It'll stop on my end too."

I want to tug his raincoat hood down and pull him into the rain. I want the water to slip under the lip of his collar and travel along his skin down to his socks. His torso is square, the shape and substance of his chest totally legible through his clothes. He doesn't have ribs that would jab me, his muscles and fat cover them too well.

"What part was your mistake?" My boldness surprises me. I find a corner of his neck to make eye contact with and stand in the question. There's a part of me that wishes I didn't ask what I just asked, because if I stay with him here, in this belief, maybe nothing does change. Maybe we return to some vague, unconsummated warmth, where he is an important person to me and me to him. Part of me is okay to stay, while the rest readies for a huge leap. Why do I need to jump? I am so uncomfortable.

Michael, confused, embarrassed, even, tells me, "The boat. On the boat."

"What about last night!" I can't slow the words. Why do I need to hear it from him?

Michael squints, furrows his brow, slightly mad: "What?"

"Something happened, we might have, we slept together?" It's wrong from the very second it comes out of my mouth, but I say it, I put it into the air. The nausea has occupied my body so fully that I turn away to fold and puke. I spit into the ground.

Erin knew Blake was drifting. I knew Blake was not there. I knew the smell of alcohol, the sound of its movement. I knew the way cocaine baggies morphed when put through the washing machine, their plastic made harder and shinier, the Ziploc sometimes lifting and tearing. Stuck in jean pockets. The smell of it high-pitched, tinny, a music box on helium. She confused me. I always felt confused.

When my stomach is empty, I turn back and he's angry, almost shaking. "I can't tell you how disturbing that is, Lydia." I lurch forward, an inside impulse, and he steps backward. "Please don't follow. Understand this is my job."

Michael disappears into the gray, the wind, the rain, and I'm left on the ground, which has not opened up to swallow me but stood there to hold me, and I would not like to be held. I know it. I didn't sleep with him. I slept with Zeke, with his bony ribs and smooth skin and dumb mustache and crater chest, in the bunk bed below me. I stumbled back into our own room. And I really tried to believe it was Michael, decided I knew what he smelled like, tasted like, what his room looked like, and I was wrong. I don't want this knowing.

Erin knew Blake was drifting. And then Blake left, and it became harder to see where she was. I didn't know where I was either.

I sleep on the couch. I stop brushing my hair. I avoid everyone but Captain. I pick at the skin of my fingernails. There is still a square of nail polish left on my right thumb, a remnant that I try to remove, scratching at its surface. I wait for Captain in the living room, all of me shoved into one corner of the velvety armchair, but he doesn't come. At least, not on time, so I wait, reducing the nail polish to a smaller and smaller shape, trying to remember to breathe, all of my movements hard, until I remember Michael's journals. Two out of five.

Before long I'm in front of Michael's door, holding my breath, and then inside, shutting the door behind me. The air is stale and cold, as I remembered it, but the room is completely different—a match of my room with Zeke, except there are two bunk beds, one on each wall, and a small desk shoved into the corner, moving boxes of files stored underneath. A creak runs through the downstairs of the house, probably Captain, stirring or looking for me. Underneath the papers on Michael's desk are three journals, the slim leather ones I've seen him use in the field, stuffing his data sheets in between pages.

He's gone. I can't access him, not without humiliating myself, and I'm reaching and straining for access still to his thoughts. To what he really thinks about me. I open one of five first. It's filled with data sheets on the left side of the binding, cut down and taped in, while his notes on the right side summarize the day, describe sharks and attacks in thorough, nearly romantic detail, and then ask broader questions, make bigger hypotheses, and wonder about what happens next.

This job requires terrible things of me, he writes. I love one place. I have no desire to go as far as I can, to see as much variety as the world's oceans have to offer. I'm tied to the Farallons. I come back and see the same sharks, and while it's a relief every time I recognize an individual, that they've survived their yearly migration, breeding season, etc., it is brutal, too, to see animals in much worse shape than last time. Bite Size has lost real mass, his flanks withering, his new scars from breeding season like forks ran alongside and twirled in his flanks. I felt I could almost see his own blood in the water, beading off his wounds into the current.

I flip through quickly. I move through all the sharks we tagged. He was disgusted by how small the new female we tagged was, Margo, concerned about her almost-social behavior with the boat, worried she was malnourished, and hoped that the acoustic pop-up tag would show us if, his guess, she'd been spending too much time feeding along the ocean floor and less time on the surface, where the real high-fat prey are.

Journal one of five ends and I move onto the second, my excitement and dread intensifying as I arrive at Angela's death (RIP). There's no data sheet for this one, only intensely scribbled notes from the field and then more, no less frantic, notes from later in the day. Liver pushed out like her body was a toothpaste tube. Horrifying. Precise. Shark-eating spreading across orca pods? Didn't recognize these two individuals, not the group that killed Midnight 10 years ago, new and unfamiliar, a threat to these sharks and this population...

I'm looking, obviously, for myself—for our kiss, for any feeling he had toward me that day, any sensation that he believed was shared. There's only this: Mistake on boat. There are other words but they're crossed out with such a vigor that the page is indented. Mistake on boat. I keep reading. The morning after, he wrote in cursive, hypothesizing the sharks leaving would have the biggest impact on how the sea lions and elephant seals parent.

They would have easier choices to make without their biggest predator in the water. By the end of that day, his notes are darker, murkier: I have spent my life relating to animals, disappearing all human responsibility in a world that runs on a different clock, a larger scale, more blood and less remorse, a balance for all things living and even all things dead. I don't want my life, I desire theirs. What good is memory if it can't hold an experience tightly, if it can't recall exactly how small I felt that day? If it can't keep me alive?

On another page, he rants for four paragraphs about erosion at North Landing, how it's worsening to the point where elephant seal and sea lion pups will be washed into the sea during a bad storm season, which this winter and new year is supposed to bring.

The worst storms ever recorded on island, the most unrelenting rain. Another page still, he gets an idea, and my stomach drops: The sharks are scared. I have been scared. I am a man. I don't want fear. I want everything back. I will bring the sharks back with blood, material, their materials are all there. Why did we get rid of chumming when it was the best thing we could do? Go to sharks and put hands up and ask, return. They cannot deny me. . . a desperate man. Mistake on the boat. Nell disappointed.

Who's Nell? The notes read as if they're from two different men. Calm and ordered data most mornings to senseless and emotional most nights. His tone shifts from measured to desperate. To creep and find nothing is a relief. To snoop and find confirmation is disappointment, which has already started to lather my throat in concrete. Horror, too. What's the difference between suspicion and curiosity? When suspicious, you are already convinced of what you're going to find out. I thought, suspected, knew that I was a mistake to him.

Bait defrosting, he writes. Bait, cold, melting, ready. The dinner he made. The fish taken from the freezer. He fed us with the bait he uses now to lure sharks back, after the orcas killed Angela. This idea, if I've read his madness correctly, is to bait and lure the sharks back with chum. I haven't seen him take the boat, so where's he even doing this? The shoreline? Does Zeke know about this? Does Captain? Is there any reason to believe that would work? White sharks swim fast and disappear into unthinkably deep water quickly. The year Michael saw the orcas' previous kill, sharks fled hundreds of miles within hours. The sharks have moved on. No chum will bring them back.

Then, mystery lines and a rare clear thought: When can I next speak to Nell? She pleads with me to get my drinking under control, to make it public, at the very least. Again she suggests daily meditation. I miss her. I don't know if I can sustainably love another person.

"Lydia?"

I hear my name from the kitchen. I return the journals. I try to control my breathing as I open the door and slip outside, then dart, as quietly as I can, to the equipment room, where I tug at the fridge handle and stick my hand into the cold, my red hands will prove where I have not been, seasick, I yell back, "IN HERE!" There are barely any fish in the fridge. The frozen piles are small now. Has this been going on for weeks?

Captain enters the equipment room with a furrowed brow, he was just in here, where was I, and I say maybe I was in the bathroom, but I've been here, holding up my pink fingertips, I've been here. Captain obviously doesn't believe me, but it doesn't matter, because the time I spent in his journals is as if I've dreamed about Michael and woke up with the sensation that I've spent time with him. A manic, unbelievable version of him, one I don't trust. Did I ever trust him? Yes. I trusted the best version, the one halfway stored in my head.

There's a sea urchin tucked into Captain's coat. He pulls it out, delicately. Water drips off its edges. It's tiny, precious. I might be hallucinating but the blue-green spikes look like they're still moving. It's not an urchin in Captain's hand, it's a sea anemone. Softer. Squishy. The anemone wiggles in his palm, no hallucination necessary to see that this slimy flower is alive. It's probably dying. Sea anemones survive out of the water by drawing their tentacles inside their body. Run, anemone, turn inside, hide.

Michael's not reckless enough to chum in front of Zeke, right? There's a gap, sometimes, between when Zeke and Michael respectively return home. I picture the light leaving the sky, slowly, Michael hanging back in the rocks, pulling his mixture of blood, fish scales, flesh, and bones out of his bag—a cooler? He must stink, bad. Is he still speaking to Nell when he's alone? Did he ruin it? Does he meditate? How long had they been together?

Another day with Captain passes, as I am officially banished to shark watch from the lighthouse. My calves burn on our way up the hill and my mind spins. Today will end with purpose. I must confirm the Michael that exists in his notes. If I can just find the madness and confront it. It's cold. The fog makes my clothes wet. Captain sits against the concrete, digging his thumb into the flesh of his knee, binoculars down. He seems tired, worn.

Two elephant seals stand, rolling their necks up so most of their front body lifts off the ground, and press their chests against each other, bobbing their heads and oozing a shorter, louder sound. When one jabs forward, its mouth opening to snap at the other, its nose jiggles and shakes. But they are not cartoons, they are huge animals, thousands of pounds.

Another is grayer than brown. She digs her flippers into the sand and draws them up through the air, bringing an arc of sand with her. The sand lands and gathers along the nonexistent ridge of her back. Some detritus spills off the sides. The end of her flipper resembles curved fingertips as she scratches herself, a flexibility I hadn't thought possible.

I fix my binoculars now on Michael. His eyelashes make delicate shadows under his eyes, his lips are chapped, his skin flushed. He hasn't said a word to me since we fought. It physically hurts, how I destroyed the version of myself he first saw. Maybe seeing me would destroy Nell's version of him.

Waves crash, distracting me. I swing the binoculars back to the elephant seals. They don't seem to react to the water. November is now December. I don't see any babies yet on the island, which means that, by the laws of time and season here, it's not yet Christmas. I'm struck by a peculiar feeling, as if a large space has opened between my ribs, my torso made an open window. The wind rushes through me, animating nothing, only moving. I am so empty it's absurd. What does Christmas mean anymore? I have all my memories and no more expectations.

The fog creeps around the island, making our access to the water patchwork.

Captain claps me on the back and tells me we should call it early. We can barely see enough ocean to scan accurately for attacks. "There's a VHS player at the house," he says, all winky. "We've got Jaws."

"Isn't that wrong, as a shark researcher?"

Captain grunts in response. "Classic's a classic. We know better."

I should go with Captain, but I can't. I tell him I'm staying until it's dark. I'll watch the sunset. He stalls, offers to stay, but I push him, explaining that I'd like to be alone. He doesn't want to accept this, but eventually does, after making me promise that I won't let visibility get too bad before I start my descent. He gives me his flashlight, a thick and plasticky red which lands heavy in my hand.

Captain hunches his shoulders as he slowly works his way down the hill. The wind is sharp, cuts. The air is wet, soaks. A chill runs through me. I've started wearing extra layers. My neck warmer on during the day, a scarf that winds around that. A beanie underneath a trucker hat. There is an elephant seal with rounded sides, she looks swollen. Maybe pregnant. Tag #78. Elephant seal #78 is expecting a baby.

Time passes like this: I watch my pregnant friend. I count the elephant seals that fight. I watch Michael and try to glean how he's feeling. He doesn't appear to be a man on the brink of a psychic break. I catch glimpses of his notes, wondering if his dark ideas continue in journals three, four, and five. I have to stay focused and patient.

The distance from me to Michael suddenly hurts, and I am consumed with the feeling that something will soon happen, whether to me or around me. Maybe it's just the hope that the space in my torso will be filled and relieved of its emptiness. Zeke hoists his backpack on and leaves early. I watch him trek back across the island toward the houses. His face tilts up to me and I freeze as he waves. He stops and stands there for a moment. Does he remember everything about that night? Did he know how drunk I was? Did it feel strange, to him, because we'd been friends? We'd been brothers?

He points to the house, then to his mouth, pantomiming drinking. He doesn't understand anything. I shake my head no. His head tips back down, to the concrete in front of him, and he keeps walking. It's getting colder but Michael is unzipping his coat, tossing it to the side. Michael paces, then opens his backpack and pulls out large plastic bags that appear filled with blood and bones. Chum. Bright red squares. The gray clouds turn purple as the light around me slips into charcoal. I hope I don't lose my angle on him.

Michael makes his body flat against the far side of the beach, where a rock wall leads from the flats into the water, and sneaks past several sleeping elephant seals—their bodies huge and suddenly scary, when so near him. I want to yell, to stop him, to radio for Captain. I want more to see the horror confirmed, an instinct in me that rots from the inside. It's disgusting. I hope to see his bad ideas take him to the edge with his blood. I almost hope that he gets hurt and I see it.

I understand why people can't turn away from car wrecks. You can hold onto the fantasy until the very last second, that no one will get hurt, no one will die. Or, if you've already lived with the risk for years, if you've seen someone drive recklessly and avoid the crash, you might want to see it end badly for once. To validate the fear and the suspicion that this outcome was here all along.

Michael is at the edge of the water. The elephant seals have let him pass. His shoes are in the surf now. The ocean seeping into his socks. He rips open a bag at a time and dumps the chum into the water. He holds his hands at his sides and stares up into the clouds. He's praying, maybe. He's asking the universe for help. He's casting a spell. There's blood on his hands and he shoves the Ziplock bags into his pockets. His hands shake.

I understand in a wash. He has been drinking this entire time. When we saw the orcas kill Angela, his hands shook. He asked me to drive the boat. We didn't have a radio or our tagging equipment. No data sheets. We were unprepared. His breath was sour, rotten. All the details line up for me, yelling what I couldn't see before.

I have to leave the lighthouse. I could puke. I miss Captain. I miss warmth. I wish I didn't need to know what I did. Hurried, I hustle to the first railing. The next step I take collides me with a soft and moving object. I scream. The blurry form of a mouse scuttles away. For a moment I expect that this scream will get Michael to turn around, to find me, but he has disappeared into a thick sort of mist, a fog that reaches into the space between us and fills it. My chest still empty. My mom still gone.

The kitchen lights have never been so caustic. Zeke sits at the table, his demeanor aggressively blank, eating trail mix from a disposable bowl. He's stopped trying to talk to me, having adopted my awkwardness as his own. The days drone on, me on the hill with Captain, him in the flats with Michael. Sometimes I cook, sometimes I don't, and these decisions go without comment. Everyone goes to bed early. I found alcohol in the freezer, packs and packs of frozen hard alcohol and mixed drinks, mislabeled, of questionable age, and I've been drinking it some nights as I sink into the couch, sucking on the still-frozen chunks.

In our living room there is one couch and one chair, the couch weathered by years of having two dogs. Last year our dogs died, one just months after the other. There's still hair ground into the corners, strands of it caught under the fabric-covered buttons, scratch marks across the arms. When Blake was sober, she cared deeply about fluffing the pillows after anyone got up from the couch. Erin didn't care about the pillows. She liked when the couch looked "lived in." A house is for living! She was arguing a case. She couldn't convince Blake of it.

This trip isn't what I thought it was and no one seems to care. Captain knows that Michael has been drinking. To what extent, I don't know. Zeke's mind, how much he's aware of, here, is mysterious to me. A part of me wants to pull his perspective closer to mine, to bring him down into the muck, into my disillusionment. If he sees the full darkness of what Michael is up to, the true absurdity, maybe I won't be so alone. My head pounds.

"When you leave the colony tonight, go back to see what Michael does alone," I tell him. I can't eat breakfast. My stomach can't do it, can't even look at it. I sip a mug of lukewarm water. "Don't let him see you."

Zeke's eyes like heavy circles of fat, sinking into his cheeks. "What the fuck?"

"Trust me."

A force pushes at my skull, willing my body into a curve. If I follow the shape, bending into it, I feel I will sit down and never get back up. To stay standing is to hold my breath, then to breathe deeply, to remind myself that I am not having a heart attack, it's just my chest pounding, the blood moving aggressively through me.

The landscape is souring to our presence here. I stare out the window into the shape of gray. Doesn't the fog make research dangerous?

"Do you understand how confusing you are?" Zeke asks, his voice with an edge.

I'm quiet. We sit there. Then, at some interval of time specific to him but not to me, he gets up, leaving his plastic bowl in the sink for me to wash. The door opens and shuts. Did he really think that we were something? That I liked him? Was flirting with him? Have I been traveling on roads predetermined for me, taking steps that I didn't know were tied to conclusions? Michael lets me on the trip; Zeke lets me close. I feel impossibly stupid.

When Captain shows up, he checks there's no one in the house before he speaks, harshly, the words covered in sand. "Get yourself together, kid. You look bad." He tells me that I need water. I say, "I'm hydrating." He's frustrated with me. Not that kind of water. I don't want to go to the boat, and it's so foggy we'll barely be able to see our own feet, but Captain insists, telling me that there's a surprise waiting for me, and I don't have the spiritual strength to refuse. It's a job, it's a job, it's a job. Act like it, Lydia. Act like it.

Captain doesn't slow for me today. His knees are in perfect working condition and his pace is swift. I sweat and follow. At least there's relief from the switchbacks up lighthouse hill. Does Michael know we're taking the boat out? Captain at the controls, he pushes us slowly north in a counterclockwise arc around the island, bringing us past Sugarloaf on to Maintop Bay, where we sway in calm waters.

On the boat, time passes slowly. I remember to breathe. I find red black in my closed eyes. Captain and I don't speak. The fog hides the surface of the water from us as we peer down from the boat. When I stand bow side, I can't see him at the stern. There are no sharks. When we break to eat, I still can't force food into my body. I can't forget how Michael looked at me, how his face dropped. There was anger on his side, and humiliation on mine, and then there was embarrassment and horror on his, and nothing at all on mine. Missing was care, love, affection, closeness. Captain tells me

I must eat. I glare at him, he's no parent to me. I can't eat. I don't feel well. He says he's sure that I don't.

"He's off the wagon," he says. "It doesn't excuse you."

What the fuck? I'm so angry I breathe through my teeth as I tell Captain the truth, that Michael is chumming to try to bring the sharks back. Zeke as my witness, he'll know by the end of today.

"Is that behavior excusable? Is that what a responsible boss should do? How can we follow him?"

Captain sighs. Sinks. I wonder if he had higher hopes for Michael. If he believed this time, the trip would be different. "It's not. You got two choices though. You join the madness, or you don't." He tells me that kind of sick is contagious because it's a sick that starts in your thinking. He wants to protect me, but more so wants me to protect myself.

Captain's response doesn't make any sense to me. Does he know about the kiss? He can't. If I told him, I would get him on my side. Captain loves me. When he says he wants to protect me, I believe him. I'm not ready, yet, though, to let anyone else into what exists between me and Michael, even if it's over.

"You're young," Captain says, when I don't say anything. "The world doesn't end past this place. My life is here."

"What do you mean?"

"Your world is bigger."

"What if I want my life to be here too?"

"It's not."

Exasperated, I ask him what he planned on showing me. The boat is too small to hide a surprise, and there's nothing to see in the water.

Captain tells me that we are waiting for a smell, not a sight. It's a little gross, like rotten broccoli, the funky bottom of a compost pile.

Before I can smell anything like he's describing, I hear barking. The sounds are somewhat like a dog's, they start and stop in short chunks, occupying the sound space of the upper mouth. Captain murmurs, "Sea lions." The sea lion's bark is as if the nose and the stomach could speak at the same time, deep and nasal, generated deep inside the animal and then transmitted through a very small opening. A foghorn chopped up and released in intervals. They don't sound louder than the elephant seals, but more precise, somehow. I could aim one of their sounds, fit it into a determined space.

Captain points into the fog, telling me that Michael and Zeke are stationed there today. I follow the line of his finger and try to imagine the two of them, curled around the sea lion colony, watching the sea lions and waiting for the first babies to arrive. Michael is working his way through prey, from elephant seals to sea lions, everything the white shark lives on.

Then there is a horrible new sound, so excruciating I can't place it at first. A screeching, high-pitched and painful. Captain squints into the gray, then turns so his ear faces the destination point, and then comes the second sound, followed by several others, yelps and shrieks gaining clear form as Zeke's voice. I'm scared. Zeke is screaming. Zeke is hurt.

Captain powers up the engine and hits the throttle so fast that the decoy is tugged out and the pole slips through my hands, rocketing over the edge of the boat. I picture the pole sinking, slowly tugging the flat layer of the decoy down with it.

Disoriented, I watch as the world around us remains the same. I can feel the cold fog rushing past my arms but I can see nothing reflecting our movement, not until we've made it to the crane. As we lift through the air, Captain tells me, "Be ready to go. You know what go mode is?"

"I think so?" Captain takes off his hat, smooths his hands over his bald head, and puts the cap back on.

"All I need you to say is, 'yes.'" I say yes.

Back on land, Captain tells me to get the med kit from the house, then take the path to the right and use my ears. I run, my hungover body working on adrenaline and fear, no other fuel, sweating through the cold. I make it to the house, which becomes a blur as I run through it in my dirty shoes, pulling the med kit out of the supply room and shoving it in a bag, which I attach to my back and tighten until my stomach overflows across the strap. Then I am running again, going right, listening to the birds and the waves, listening for Zeke's pain so I find him and help, so I find them and learn what happened.

I stop and allow myself to hinge over. The ground is dirt and gravel. I spit into the dirt. My body rights itself. Survival is back on. I breathe through my mouth. The island curves up and down. The sea lions start to bark, I go to the right and that's when I hear him. Zeke's long groan. Around him, the worried shouts of Michael and Captain.

Captain and Michael have Zeke stretched across their shoulders. His face is all pain. I search him for what's wrong. Captain and Michael tug him forward, but he doesn't move, yelping, asking them to please stop. I yell that I am here, I hold up the med kit in my arms, and

I step closer, crouching down as I maintain balance at the beginning of rocks, where the ground grows brittle and holey. Zeke's ankle has gotten lodged between two rocks and there is blood all around. The rocks have torn through his wool socks. His ankle is cut deep. There's not only blood but fat and, an internal screaming, bone, too. I feel nauseated. They're not seeing what I do, a bad fucking injury. A serious accident.

"Stop!" I yell. "He's stuck!" Captain and Michael, barely seeing me, stop, and Captain tells me to switch with him, so I assume Zeke's weight and Captain stoops to Zeke's foot. He murmurs that I was right, and he starts to work Zeke's ankle out of its stuck place. Blood stains his hands red.

The waves get louder. We're on the edge of Emperor's Bathtub, an area of rocks that dips down into a large rectangular pool of turquoise water and closes it off on the sides, making a natural bathtub. Layers of water rush over the furthest rock wall and into the bathtub, flooding the air with mist. Zeke could have fallen into the water, been swept out to sea.

The entire right side of my face itches as I realize Michael and I are sharing Zeke's body. He wears dark sunglasses, his skin the normal crisped pink, his hair greased and underneath a hat, bits that escape the hat tucked behind his ears. He is pale again, almost sickly. Drunk or hungover.

Zeke yelps and I am gross, shame running through me, in Zeke's crisis, when he is literally bleeding, I find Michael. Quickly, I adjust and recommit to the present moment, the actual, and Zeke's foot slides out of the rocks, held on each side by Captain. Michael's rain jacket comes off, then his fleece, then his long sleeved shirt, and this long sleeved shirt, a stretchy material, passed down to Captain, who wraps it around Zeke's shoulders. Captain pushes gauze from the med kit to Zeke's ankle and spins medical tape around it in tight circles. He's trying to stop the bleeding.

Then the four of us are teetering back to the house. Is Zeke afraid? He sweats into my shoulder as I try to hold my part of his weight, making invisible the strain it takes my body. There is no such strain in Michael, or in Captain, and I don't know why Captain didn't step in to assume Zeke's other half, instead rushing ahead on the path, but I trust Captain, filled with a strange knowing that Captain makes good choices, that he considers other people, that he has a handle on his place in the world. My shoulders expand under Zeke's mass. My arms strengthen. My hips even out at the sides, pushing my torso wider. My feet grow. A mouse loops through my legs, I try to hold in my flinch. Maybe two, or the fog is doubling them. A tiny squeaking.

We become a set of crutches, me left and Michael right. Zeke uses his good leg to hop. The path creeps on. I hold my side tight. Zeke, his armpit leaking into me, smells like my deodorant. He didn't use to smell like that.

It was hard enough to run through this fog as a single body. As a body of three, it's even harder. We move fast but deliberate, as precise as we can, and every few feet there's a miscalculated step that throws our triangle off balance. We can't fully see the ground—only in quick flashes as patches of fog blow by, revealing what's underneath us— but we must walk as if we do.

Because we can't see the ground, we don't see the mouse holes, and Zeke's right foot hits one, bad, his ankle jutting out at a perpendicular angle, the healthy one, but healthy ankles aren't supposed to bend that direction, even the best ankles would have a hard time handling this shape, and he groans, and we slow to regain our grip. When we slow, a bleary slab of fog rushes by and the ground comes into quick focus, except it doesn't, the dirt moves as an undulating mass. I can't understand what is moving.

There, the twin houses on the horizon, now close to us. As we move Zeke and hoist halfway through the doorframe, I realize the squirming hillside was mice, mice scurrying in and out of their burrows, mice moving so quickly they are indiscernible from the path and the path from them. The ground, what I thought was the ground, was mice.

The worst part was Blake had been gone for a long time before we knew what happened to her, which meant we waited to find out what happened to us. Blake had been gone a long time. What was a long time? Three days was a year. Two weeks was a lifetime. Erin's hair fell out. I stopped sleeping.

This island doesn't feel so far from the world anymore. The city is just 27 miles across water. There are people over there who love me, who think of me. Here I wanted to see if everything would stop.

Erin and Blake met when they were thirty and thirty-three. They were living in San Francisco. Blake grew up there, in a strange house in the outer Sunset, where it gets real foggy. The house was light green and had a massive clock fixed to the wall above the stairs. Erin had moved to the city from the East Coast a few years earlier for a job. Blake was tall, with long and curly hair, taken to wearing big, bold-printed sweaters. Erin was short and blonde, often in mom jeans, turtlenecks, and blazers. These images of them come from photos, mostly, and a few home videos. I try to picture them as strangers in the world, plucked apart from each other.

All of Blake's friends were lesbians too, and most of them worked low-paying jobs or went to school to hopefully gain higher-paying jobs, frequenting their friends' apartments and the lesbian dive bars that used to exist in the city on the weekend. Erin didn't know that she was a lesbian, necessarily, she had dated men and that was fine, but nothing had worked out. It was in San Francisco, at a bar called Amelia's in the Mission, that my moms met and fell in love over a slow burning ten months that threatened to demolish Erin.

Way later, Blake had been sober for a long time. What's a long time? Between my years of six and fifteen. When she relapsed, I met a shadow version of my mom I had only shallow memories of. There was a new person in the room. Blake had lots of rules before, things were very defined, rigid, even, and had fewer after, and the rules she kept came with lots of exceptions, jagged at the edges. At first, I thought she was more fun, that a sudden and remarkable flexibility had rushed in, a wind I was grateful for.

They took me on a trip up the coast for my sixteenth birthday. Blake wanted to drive the blue 1971 Lotus Elan she'd finally fixed up after years of it sitting in the garage. The Lotus was a two-seater convertible, skinny and low to the ground, you can feel all the bumps when you go over it. It's a little car, cute and slick. Before I was born, Blake helped a guy who ran a junkyard in Alameda for extra cash and car parts for years. The Lotus was his pride and joy, always kept in the shade or under a cover when it rained. Eventually he told her she could buy the Lotus off him for cheap. He liked her, and the suspension was busted anyway, the car frame rotting in several spots, so it'd take a lot of extra work to get it running again.

Erin fought her on it, because two-seater, because the only way to get three people into that little car is to sit one person on the middle of the back, where the top comes down. I'd done it plenty of times coming back from basketball practice with a friend, but never on the freeway, not for long drives. Blake was convinced, though, and pushed until Erin gave in.

When we climbed into the car, I beat Erin to the bonus spot, and looped my legs under the back of their seats so that I could keep myself in place. Blake blasted the heat. We set off. The wind pushed my hair into my eyes, out in sharp lines behind me, and back. The tips of my ears grew cold. As we headed down Marin, I threw my arms up like we were riding a rollercoaster, which made Erin laugh and Blake grin. I stretched my fingertips so that the heat touched them.Erin put on an old CD of Blake's, Elton John, and the music was loud, and the wind louder as we sped down the curves through Albany. When we got onto the freeway, the water sparkled and the air grew colder and the sun was stronger, the heat still whooshing through the little car. I felt the force of Blake's acceleration push me back, my shins and feet flexed, holding me into place, my little hooks under my moms' seats.

Then we were flying, and the wind seemed to be beating me, and I felt it in my abs then, needing the rest of my muscles to sit back up, to hold on, to not fold and flap into the wind. The music, loud, I felt myself sway to it, and the cold and hot air mixed, and I smiled, laughing, and then there were other sounds: Erin yelling at Blake, telling her to slow down, her hand reaching for me, my feet slipping from underneath the seats, the orange speed dial rolling over one hundred, Blake's eyes shining, saying, "It's a sports car! You drive it like a sports car!"

And Erin spitting back, "Not when our kid's barely attached to it!"

Erin's worry, how it filled her face, how her hands were desperately moving to slow Blake and to secure me, it changed the sound of the music, made it scary and overwhelming, and my laughter left my chest, fear filling the remaining space, and my head tipped back further and further, and I started to yell STOP and that got Blake to turn around, and in a second I saw concern flash across her, and the car slowed, too fast, my body bending and slamming forward into the two seats, Erin screaming now, and I was floating, floating, I stayed in the car but I was floating, and my moms couldn't keep me safe from the wind anymore.

It was no longer fun and a seed of something else was planted in me, that what is fun can also hurt, and that I could fly out into the wind and get swallowed up. My own parent, who for so long had all the rules in the world to not hurt herself or others, could hurt me.

When Blake couldn't get another job in tech, she wrote to everyone she'd ever worked for. Erin helped her make a LinkedIn page, and there was a glossy photo of her face advertising her availability to everyone who clicked. But everything that was offered to her would have meant taking a cut in title and pay, and Blake's pride was too big, so she used the free time to develop an idea for a startup that was always shifting. An online marketplace for used power tools, an Uber for taxi drivers that lowered the prices of rides if you bought a bunch of rides at once, an opensource Jstor with a social feed, like a Letterboxd for academics, but these ideas weren't very good at making money. That was the missing bit, money.

The specifics don't matter because there were never specifics that stuck, just facts that spun out into the air and asked for everything. It was easy to believe her, but the dread never left my stomach. Soon she started taking jobs in our neighborhood restoring stained glass windows. I remember the blue crayon she kept in her shirt pocket, used to rub out a wax outline of the original window design, which she did if she had to take it apart and put it back together again, and I remember the way she shaved off the cement with a box cutter, all her attention on the fragile glass in front of her. She took care of the windows she restored. I never saw a single piece break.

We never played music in our house but when Blake came home buzzing we did, the stereo under the TV blasting so loud the edges got staticky, the old machine putting music and fun into a room that didn't exactly feel fun. It was a risky fun, a balancing game that we knew wouldn't end well, but you had two choices, one, anticipate the pieces falling and breaking on the ground and feel the break as if already broken (wait), or two, pretend the break was not coming and dance (ignore). Two was more fun than one, even if it meant the break hurt more.

When Blake left, she'd taken a new job, three months in at the geothermal power plant outside of the city. California wanted more and more of the state's energy to come from renewables, and the plant needed more skilled workers. It was salaried and stable and physical. She didn't talk much about the job, except once to describe the smell of the steam and how it stuck to her clothes. I asked how big the turbines were, how hot the steam got, how many women worked with her. Did she like the job as much as restoring old windows? Did she enjoy it like she used to enjoy carpentry? She didn't answer me.

For a long time Blake was drifting and Erin saw her moving as if in slow motion. I wasn't like Erin, I didn't know where, only that Blake was often not here, not as close as I wanted her to be. Blake had been leaving, always leaving. It was my senior year. I got into Cal! We celebrated with cake and the chocolate was bitter in my mouth. Erin's head kept turning out of the room. Blake left on a short walk that lasted an hour. We went out to dinner. Blake slipped into the bathroom and missed all the bread at the beginning. Erin made a toast, told me she was proud of me. Tasia snuck in a flask and got so emotional she cried.

"I feel like Erin's always looking for Blake," Tasia said, pushing her index finger into her forehead. She got migraines and they were bad when she drank, but she drank anyway. She bent her finger and pushed the knuckle into the skin. Opposite to how I felt drunk, all my pain removed.

"Yeah, I guess," I said. I wanted to say to Tasia that Erin was worried about Blake's health, and the sick I hoped to mean was easily curable and not lethal, solely in the body, not shared across the body and brain, like, she has Lyme disease, the short kind, or a kidney stone, or a tumor that turns out to be benign.

In July Blake left and Erin told me it was so she could get some space, and in August Erin told me she didn't know where Blake was, and the police didn't know either. Suddenly Blake's absence had become a disappearance. Blake was missing, not the type of missing that ends in the way you know it's going to. Before, her missing had been predictable, i.e., if she was going on a long walk, she was coming back speaking so fast her jaw rumbled, if she was coming home late from a work trip she was blasting music, if she was blasting music she was high, etc.; there were patterns to the ways she left and came back.

Blake flew to visit her sister in D.C., but Aunt M. told us that one night she didn't come home. Phone calls went to voicemail. The last place she was seen was at a sports bar, emerging into the muted lights of a busy D.C. street past midnight.

Blake was distinctive. She no longer had the long curly hair, but she had a brash streak of gray in the front of her short cut, and a tattoo on her right hand. She was gone for six weeks, more precisely forty-seven days. It wasn't entirely quiet. Sometimes she'd call Erin, I could tell, because Erin's shoulders curved down as she got up and left the room, pushing the phone to her ear, her hand to the phone. "I'm here," she'd say. "Shhh, I'm here. Please stay on with me. Please keep talking." I sent her a few texts but in general I was too angry.

When I tell the story of my moms, I often focus on their second lives with each other. They met in their thirties and had me barely tipped into their forties. They lived a whole life before me. They wanted me badly. If two women decide to have a baby, they must explain themselves over and over again as potential parents. Having a baby requires planning and risk, wild belief and determination. I was the result of that. They knew themselves before they had me. How can all that still be true? They were supposed to be fully formed, figured out, complete. They were supposed to be good moms.

It's hard to overdose on cocaine. Barely anyone, say, snorts it until their heart stops. But it's easy to accidentally OD when it's cut with fentanyl. I follow a girl who kept posting about harm reduction, harm reduction, harm reduction, who posted stories about how twelve-step programs are life-saving but not a catch-all net, some people keep using and we can keep them alive, who passed out Narcan for free, plastic contraptions with emergency medicine that you can shoot up someone's nose when their lips are turning blue, who preached about the effectiveness of testing your drugs before using. I tried to imagine my mom taking a pinch of coke and testing it, waiting until the results came out, tossing the bad drugs. I couldn't. I didn't text her but I picked up a free kit for myself and kept the Narcan in my backpack, everywhere I went.

She OD'd, accidentally, barely any coke in her system, in some room in a place I don't know, far away from me and Erin, too far to be reached, too far to be asked to stay and to say yes. There was not a danger for her with us and yet she left, there was no reason for her not to mother, and yet.

If I saw the room, would I remember its parts forever? Would I want to make it lighter, brighter, softer, easier?

I say, my mom died, my mom died, my mom died. They say, Was she the one who carried you? I don't want to answer their question. My mom died, I repeat. She danced when she was mad and she taught me how to clean a bathroom. She would have liked that I got this job. Her love for herself was conditional, which meant that her love for everyone else was conditional, too, but when the conditions were right it was like standing in the direct sun.

Her love connected me to the world and back. She taught me how to hang a frame, how to fix a broken pipe, how to assemble a bed from scratch, how to cut glass for a stained-glass window. Everything about how she lived was impractical, but she was the most practical person I ever knew. I knew her. I didn't understand her, but I knew her.

I never saw the way she did coke, only after. I never saw her snort a line, rub it into her gums, whatever you do. The action itself was missing. I saw her enter rooms and leave them. I didn't know what they looked like inside.

Zeke groans. His eyebrows push into each other, his eyes blank but unmoving, fixed on some random point ahead of him. He contains himself. There's nothing moving across his face except for the occasional tightening of his jaw muscles, a blinking that lasts a second too long, eyelids heavy. He sinks into the thrifted purple armchair. His ankle is propped on a milk crate, the wound wrapped in cotton gauze, blood leaking slowly through the bandage.

Captain has brought out the board game with the missing pieces, Sorry!, with fewer apologies. We have lit candles, not because the power's out, but maybe it feels like it should be. No matter how much water I drink, my mouth is dry.

Zeke's in pain. Michael's clearly nervous, his movements jittery, his patience thin. He stands up and sits down, his chair unable to hold him. He paces. It's windy tonight, the sounds outside loud, nearly louder than they've been this whole time, but perhaps it's just the adrenaline of the accident, constructing a storm out of everything. Michael leaves the room to make a satellite call and the cushion of his orange chair wilts in place. I draw a Sorry! card and replace one of Captain's pieces with my own. He grumbles and assesses the board.

"You wanna draw or we'll draw for you?" Captain asks Zeke, breaking his concentration. His index finger misses his thumb.

Zeke winces. "I'll draw." Zeke hinges forward and pulls a card. Five spaces. I offer my arm and he nods. I move his piece along as he slouches back into the chair. Captain studies his positions on the board, then throws a glance to the hallway, where Michael disappeared.

"Don't fucking cheat." Pushing himself up by the arms, the table wobbles and the pieces follow. I nod, Zeke nods. A serious response to a real question. Captain leaves to the hallway. If my ears strain, they can suss out Michael's voice but not his words. A negotiation is underway.

Alone, Zeke addresses me in a whisper, "Should I tell my parents yet?"

Parents don't exist here. His parents, and their place in his words and thoughts, rattle me. It's as if I can hear them whispering and worrying, filling the space around him, fretting over him, debating how and when they'll get him to a hospital. Parents don't live here. "I don't know that they want me to," he says. "The last time things went wrong here, the shark program got totally fucked."

"Didn't they lose a boat?" I say, cutting him off, knowing the story. The sailboat that a rich donor had leant to the program, the journalist who snuck off the vessel one stormy night only to wake to it galloping across the waves with nobody on board. MARO felt Michael was responsible because he allowed the journalist to stay on the sailboat alone, responsible too for allowing her to leave it unmanned. When marine salvagers found the boat, they found battered wood, damages in the thousands, hundreds of miles from where it slipped its anchor. The shark program was almost dead in the water.

"Isn't this worse? Isn't this all worse?" Zeke swallows, his lips chapped. "You know, it's MARO who gives us the funding, and Fish & Wildlife, but it's Michael who writes the grants, Michael who gets the money, Michael who hires us. It all goes through him."

The blood on Zeke's ankle is darker now, the gauze soaked, and this progression makes me nervous, jolting me. My answer, it depends on what happens to his ankle. Yes, losing an ankle is worse than losing a boat. Alleged drunk sex is worse than losing a boat. What about a kiss on a boat? Michael has jumped off the deck of observer and into the mix of the natural world.

It's disorienting to dream up the depths of how bad Zeke's injury could be. That's what's dizzying here, in that his injury could be nothing serious, a set of stitches, an easy recovery. My arm bled more when it was cut, a steady stream, the elbow crease a junction of major veins and potential disaster zones. There was no glass stuck inside, and the wound was cleaned quickly.

I still went to physical therapy, massaged a block of scar tissue for months until it dissolved. The result of my arm being mostly fine, how much did this depend on the speed of care? Other people lifted my arm, wrapping it in towels, pressed their hands into the fabric, keeping the blood inside, placed me on a stretcher, rushed under bright lights, to a hospital, where I was looked at inside, and finding nothing, the doctor made a wide red mouth into an even surface of skin again.

"Should I change the dressing?" We're still alone. Kids who broke a precious object and have to fix it. He's older than me, but now that he's hurt, is made someone who calls his parents or doesn't, pushing us back into the same category. Almost—

A trickle of blood wiggles free of the gauze and down the tan flat of his foot. I'm already moving to the kitchen by the time he says yes, where I grab the med kit from the table, looping the bottle of rubbing alcohol in between my thumb and index fingers and pinching a clean rag with my remaining. He looks woozy in his pink chair when I'm back, the wrong sort of throne, and I've never seen him so tender and needy, unable to front that he's holding himself together, his face sweating, Zeke, a raw level of fear and uncertainty surfaced. I can see his bones and that he's afraid, and I'm still in the room with him. Don't worry, I tell him, it will all be fine. He is unconvinced. He doesn't want to see it again.

"So don't look!"

"Don't fuck it up though."

I glare at him. "You'll either see me fuck it up or see me do a good job." He dramatically throws a hand over his eyes and forehead.

"Just do it."

I peel off the gauze and press the clean rag to the surface of the wound—not really a surface, more so a window with bars over the glass, fucking unsettling, reaching into a room when a tabletop is expected. I fall into his leg, into this wound. I glance at his face, eyes still closed, cheeks squeezing upwards now, the open room of his leg somewhere that hurts, obviously, okay, I'm looking at it again, and my hand applies pressure while the other shakes alcohol into a large cotton square and removes the rag and dabs at it, the blood and muscle red, the bone behind it white and impossibly sturdy. I'm embarrassed for the bone and that it can be seen. I take another bottle of alcohol and squeeze to spray from a foot removed, and he peeks at me.

"BRO! What the hell! What's taking you so long!"

"OK! GOD!"

I take a new cut of gauze and press the fabric over the wound and tape the sides, cutting the edges clean. The gauze feels flimsy, the whole project of redressing—of dressing it, of keeping it contained—too huge for us. I tell Zeke it's done. There he is, vulnerable and hurting and small. Does his wound itch? What kind of dis-comfort is he in? There's no hydrocodone on this island, only extra-strength Tylenol. Sometimes I can look at people and see that they were also kids once and that they'll die someday. I can see they're hurt and I want to make them feel better. Even though they hurt me, I'd like to keep them around.

"Do you remember? The night we—?"

"Of course," Zeke bristles. "Even though you clearly wish it didn't happen."

This accusation hangs for a second, because it's true. But in accepting that, an additional injury will be confirmed. He is right that I was wrong.

"I was really drunk."

"So was I."

"I don't remember all of it."

This fact almost registers with him, like he stutters in his stubbornness, but only for a moment. "It was really fun, though. Right? I mean, I asked, and you said yes, and then the next day you completely blew me off."

"I just—I thought we were friends." I swallow, steel myself. "I wanted to be your friend."

He softens there, and tells me, "Of course we're friends. We were friends first. And we can be whatever you want."

"I don't want you to see me like that."

He sighs, then, an exhausting sigh, and tells me he doesn't think there's anything wrong with how he sees me. He asks for acknowledgement, acknowledgement that it was easy, whatever was between us, that it was easy and good. I can feel my body sliding away from me, its edges blurring, moving me into a place away from the present. I like Zeke. I admire him. I want to be his friend, and I thought we were even more than that, not romantic, but familial. I thought he saw himself in me. I thought, I thought, I thought. I can't see myself.

There are footsteps in the hallway. The men come back with a plan. They will send a helicopter. Zeke will be saved, whisked back to the real world where we have the manpower and technology to save ankles and repair broken skin. When? Michael and Captain chew on their lips. They don't know. The storm won't stop, obscuring the sky from helicopters and the water from boats. The sound of the rain gets louder, a dull pounding. The rhythm changing. The glass gaining moisture, us fogging the window from the inside.

"I think I need to call my parents," Zeke says. Michael and Captain swivel their heads to glare at him. Captain doesn't want him to, says they'll know he's coming back on a med evac, but Zeke says it's better if he talks to them himself because they're going to freak out and hearing his voice will help keep them calm. I pray to disappear.

"I'm worried about what it will do to the program," Michael says, biting his nails. I've never seen him do that before. Captain isn't talking. Zeke's fingers move faster now along his thumb, growing more and more distressed. Michael shoves his whole thumb into his mouth. Captain starts to pace. Zeke tries to reposition his leg but it hurts and he stops. Captain pours him a cup of water. Zeke tries to find me now, but I am somewhere else, not findable. I have sunken past the first layer of my skin.

Yes, Zeke's ankle is an open door, and our supervisors want to keep him in his chair, which they, bigger and stronger, can probably do, but Zeke is fighting his way out of the room, reaching for people who exist in the world and love him. On water and land, he has two alive parents. He never missed his weekly satellite call, and he once read me an email from his dad, detailing how a tree in their yard was starting to grow into the powerline, the roots interfering with their electricity. He was willing to do everything he could to save it. To keep the house's power without sacrificing a tree, without registering a loss that all the roots of nearby trees would feel too. "My son, what can we do? This is your world of expertise. Please advise. Love." Everything around me slows. The house and its air are room temperature butter, melting but appearing stable. Holds form but easily smeared.

I launch up from the chair and across the room, walking or running to the door, and I hear the shouts of the men reaching for me but I ignore them and open the door and meet the storm, face to face, and run around the edge of the house and down the side of the hill, where there is no path, where the fog can hide me, where the ghosts are loudest and I am the most and the least alone. In winding lines that run roughly parallel to the path, mice scurry, making shapes in the dirt as they move. This many mice, moving in the daylight, unconcerned that I can see them, not afraid, not even aware.

The unsettling part is that the mice have made a decision to congregate, a decision to move together as a group, a decision to grow into a huge group, etc., and so on, and I watch, as though watching someone pack all the things in their house in preparation for an earthquake. Do they know that poison is coming? Do they know that someone or something is trying to kill them all?

Within the first year of her relapse, Blake suddenly believed in ghosts. Inexplicably, as someone who previously thought life simply and cleanly ended after death. She began to describe presences in our house, energetic ones, and claimed to see shadowy figures lurking in the corner of our kitchen in the middle of the night. The trick, she'd tell me, was to set a hard line with the spirits. "Don't start a dialogue," she said to me. "And if they try to start one with you, make it clear—this is my house now, and I'm not interested in talking to you." She tried to problem-solve the evil she felt, but it didn't work, her boundaries not solid enough to keep the bad at bay. What if I let in all the bad now, what if I let in everything, start talking to any presence I can find out here? Would she be included?

The seals are waiting for me, scattered across the rocks, the waves spitting over them. I sit too close, shivering, watching, waiting for anything to happen. I can see the elephant seals without my binoculars, I am so close. I'm cold, my hair is starting to dampen, and I wonder if anyone is coming after me. Zeke's ankle is fucked and he won't be able to walk. Michael is a coward. Captain trusts me. I don't know why I came here, except the gap in my chest opened again and I couldn't sit in the empty space. I close my eyes. I see a blue like the manufactured color of the Lotus. My chest hurts. My ribs pull against my sides.

When I open, there's a ripple along the back of an elephant seal down the rocks, close to the beach. She is gray-brown, the seal I've seen take elegant sand baths with the edge of her flippers. She shimmies along, rocking her body forward, making an unfamiliar grunt, this one deeper and softer, not a sound meant to connect to other creatures. At the end of her body, where there's a tail like a shrimp's, rooted at a base with two flippers that spread out from it, a mass pushes its way through, then opens its mouth. It is the rounded head of an elephant seal pup, the pink inside of its mouth visible.

She's a mom! I want to yell. I whip my head around and I'm alone. She's a mom! I yell, but the sound is swarmed by the birds' squawking and the yelling of the other seals. It's loud here, so loud, and I am quiet. It's #78, it must be, I know her. It's my friend and she's a mom. My friend is a mother!

The baby opens and closes its mouth like Pac-Man, its tongue thick and pink, searching for air, searching for what's outside. As the mom wriggles forward, the baby's face is pushed against the rocky beach. What must it feel like, to be the baby seal? To emerge from what is warm and soft to the smear of rocks in your face? But the baby's face is serene, its eyes still closed, its mouth now closed, the neck emerging, as if it trusts this movement. On its neck there is legible fur, matted from the liquid inside. Shining, the baby twists out slowly, then all in a sudden lump, its flippers springing from where they were pinned at its sides. The mom is tired. Her flippers hang over the seal's neck and head as her baby breathes, its face turned away from me.

Everything is still. Deep in my gap, nestled between the ribs on the right side, there is a pain, a bruising, a soft place pushed hard.

Then the mom pushes ahead on her flippers and starts to rotate around so that she faces her baby. As she moves, a bright red bloom slides out of her end, the afterbirth, which looks shiny and vivid enough to be its own organ, still alive. The mom puts her nose to the baby's skin and sniffs. The baby stirs and its eyes expand into large black circles. The mom opens her mouth, a triangle with rounded edges on the sides, and calls out, loud. The baby, not facing its mom, automatically responds. And the two call like that, back and forth, squawking, wheezing, yelling, until the birds start to gather.

In Michael's notes on my notes, back when we were looking at sharks, he told me I could be more descriptive using fewer words. This comment seemed misleading to me, asking my hands to tie themselves in a knot. Now, staring at the elephant seals laid out over the rocky beach, wiggling out of the ocean, yelling into the mist, I see he was trying to get me to take myself out of it. He's wrong, though. He may have identified the problem, but his answer is to pretend we have some control over the fact of our observation. If I am looking at you, I can't squint my eyes and pretend I am seeing through some other opening.

The birds gather around them, but skitter close to the baby, to its tail, to where, I can now see, there are pink bits of placenta stuck, and what looks like an umbilical cord—the birds pull at the placenta and the chord. The mom yells, roars, keeping her mouth open and moving from side to side. The birds hop back, scared. Then dart in again. The placenta keeps sliding out of the mom, and as she moves around, her underbelly grows red with blood. Finally, with the right movement, a lucky gull grabs the edge of the placenta and pulls its filmy shape out from underneath the mom, and the mom yells and belches as the gulls hop away, down the rocks, where the birds fight over it amongst themselves, and the baby screams because the mom is screaming.

When Zeke and I went swimming with Captain, the water was filled with sea lions, so many the water literally felt crowded. They were not scared. The gulls squawk and scream as they pull apart the placenta, and soon there is nothing except more bloodstained rocks where it used to be.

I wonder what kind of mother Blake would have been, if she had not grown consumed with dying herself.

The sun breaks through the clouds and then the clouds wash back over it. The rain spits in patches now, drops whirled this way and that. Mice run around and over my feet, their bodies brushing the sides of my legs. I twitch, scream, push them away. It gets darker and no one comes for me. I lay on my back, shoving my hands into my armpits again, where there are concentrated pockets of heat, my jaw chattering, listening to the elephant seals bark, wondering if one will make it to my stretch of beach and accidentally squash me. I fall asleep with the elephant seals.

When I wake up, much of the herd are gone. The sky is somewhat orange, and I am curled into a half-moon, my clothes soaking wet. I don't know how long I napped for, probably not more than fifteen minutes or so, but it feels different here. There's a sound I haven't heard yet, a buzzing, mechanical wind. It starts distant and grows closer, sending a vibration through the ground that reaches into my body. This is the earthquake the mice have been waiting for. Does the shaking send them further into the ground or up to the surface?

The sound gets a shape when I see them. A pair of helicopters, black blurs in the sky, tangled knots of insects held together into solid masses. The rumble roots in my stomach and splits my ribs further. My mom still dead. The empty space growing.

Pellets drop through the sky, a correction to my flash of hope, tiny at first and then growing in size toward the ground, light, a steady pitter patter of pellets hitting all around me. I pick one up, let it roll from left to right in the center of my palm. They remind me of the pellets we'd buy as a family at the Little Farm in Berkeley, dried out circles the goats ate from the palm of my hand, tickling me, making me laugh. Blake always brought vegetables to feed the animals, stalks of celery and bunches of romaine lettuce. When she stuck a piece of celery through the fence, at about my eye-line, she gestured to her ear and told me to listen. I couldn't hear when the goats ate the pellets, but with the vegetables there was a series of crunches, truly great, me gripping the fence posts and getting close enough to listen without becoming something to chew on. I heard a snapping, mushing, swallowing. The goat's ears flicking and nose pushing through the gap in the fence, once the food was gone. I was four or five.

I pick up two, three, four, five. I fill my fists with them and roll them around my palms. I tilt my face up to the sky and let them hit my face. The air is gray with falling pellets. It doesn't sound like rain. It's not anything I've heard before. And I wonder if this sound will fill the empty space in my chest, if it will rejoin my ribs, if it will fill my stomach, I can't remember the last time I ate or what it was. I wonder if I will ever meet Michael's wife, if I will learn the shape of her face, if her family is one of failed men like mine is of failed women, if I am a failed woman, if everyone knows or if it is just me wondering. Through the blurry gray of the pellets I see the water. I make my way to the water. The water, the ocean, the water, it will dissolve me, the water is huge, scary, beating, I shove myself in.

For a second, quiet.

The wind sifts through all surfaces. The weight of water holds my middle together, the heavy place where the biggest feelings reside. First, I feel the shift, deep cold against my toes and thighs. High pitched foam, carbonation, above my ears, a warmth, a bubbling. Then sound, catching up to the movement of water. Chirping, barking, swooshes.

If I don't rely on my sight to note the sea lion in front of me, to what do I move in response? What's faster, the speed of light or sound? The invasive mice are good for the owls, bad for the storm petrel, good for tiny crustaceans, squid, and zooplankton, bad for me. The water, it feels blue. The cold, it exists in liquid and across bodies. Darker still, there is a warm beating where reds, yellows, and whites hang, suspended. Fat, bone, blood. Kelp floats, tossed through waves, its strands like ancient hair. The clumps spin and spin.

Water cools. Blood wavers from red to blue. If you're looking at a particle, you have two choices, to know where it is, or to know how fast it's moving. If you locate it, you cannot know its velocity. If you detect its speed, you lose its place. The strange thing about physics is results live and die in the observer. How you're looking, and for what, determines what you see.

I lowered myself so my face hit the surface just below my nose. Bubbles escaped my mouth as I swam, sticking close to the top layer, its shadow. A breeze hit, pushing the surface into small-ridged mountains of water. I swam into them as they swam into me. In that moment, I became the water, had the sensation I was the water, rather it was a lack of sensation that allowed this sameness. My body lost heat, lost all differentiation. I'm sure I kept breathing, but the breath was the same as the breeze, wasn't it?

The water moved, cold and smooth. The water moved, the breeze its propellor. The water moved, the moon its engine. The birds loud. Screaming. Sharks gone.

How badly Michael didn't want things to change here. For the sharks to stay. For the sharks to return. Did he chum tonight? Will he again?

The brittle star curved over rocks and swaths of the sea floor. The water moved. The water stilled. The surface further away now. The pressure a light squeezing. And the warm breathing of my own heart, a surprise.

I am drowning and I am alive! Two things to remember for the entity that used to be me and is now the water, the brittle stars, the breeze, the gulls, the sea lions, the sharks several hundred miles away. This drowning is shared among us all, and for this reason there is the strong idea that it will hurt less, but I'm wrong.

There is I, back again, me, not us, my singularity rushing back in the form of, it hurts. The water is not calm, it storms at me, crashing over my head when I try to reach the surface, a current pulling my ankles back and sending me into a tight spiral, my body pushed further down and away, I remember the map of the Farallons, how beyond the islands the depth of the ocean leaps from three hundred feet to three thousand, the drop off unthinkably sudden and severe. I'm accelerating down like the scared shark. My body is sinking into the shallow like a stone, tossed around, and as I become heavier and sink faster, I'm reminded of Captain and his free dives, the woman he loved who died, how the pressure changes your blood chemistry. The air in my chest burns and there's a ripping under my collarbone so strong I let the air go, making my own bubbles, and I take a breath, inhaling water, filling my lungs with salt, the burning does not go away, it grows worse, but the space in my chest slowly fills. If I die, will I be a part of the ocean?

My chest burns, my space filled. Relief floods me. The tumbling has stopped, the water wild and fizzing above me. My arms reach up and I'm exhausted, full, with nothing to get me back to the light. I see my mom's face, as if she's in the ocean with me. She floats close, her curls suspended in the water. She is smiling, smiling, smiling, approaching me, and just as I brace to feel her forehead knock into my skull, she disappears over me without disappearing herself, as if her face has stretched to lay flat over and into mine.

My legs twitch. My chest no longer aches. A dark shape appears, pushing through the bubbles, swimming to me. If my mom is already with me, I don't recognize this ghost. Until his hands are under my arms and we are lifting together to the surface. It is Captain, and he is pulling me out, my chest and shoulders swelling as he does.

Soon enough my stomach is being pulled out of me, or what feels like that, everything expelled. The space in my chest emptied again. I stare at Captain's face, then the clouds, and I wonder if I am looking with my mother's eyes.

As the boat pulls away, speeding up over the waves, the water forming into a solid surface underneath us, a shark fin cuts through the foam. The islands fade, reverting into planets, massive and crunchy molars in the distance. As we pass under the Golden Gate bridge, I smell compost and rotten vegetables. Captain explained to me that we were smelling for whales that day, that's what whale breath smells like, the mist coming straight out of their nose.

Erin waits for me in the marina parking lot. I wish that Blake was standing next to her, even if she couldn't remain still, pacing in circles around Erin, exhaustion on the move. Cypress trees shake behind Erin. She plays with the chain of her necklace, pulling the clasp around to the front and back. She seems tiny. Her face, dark and worried, tells me she won't ask too many questions yet.

I have bruises on my knees and elbows from the rocks in the water. I did not go in where it's safe. I was underwater for somewhere close to four minutes. Nothing near Captain's record. I'm tired, still, like the water sunk into my skin with real weight. If I experience severe chest pain, persistent coughing, or difficulty breathing, doctors want to see me again. Turns out there's no safe patch of water for swimming around the islands. What's safe to Captain is different than what's safe for me.

Erin plays Elton John in the car as we drive back up the hill. She sold the Lotus. It was in good condition when Blake died and we needed the money. This car, bigger and safer, is black turned a sleet gray with its layer of dust. I roll my window down and stick my face into the wind. The seat buckle cuts into my lower stomach.

When a white shark hunts a sea turtle or other large prey, the prey swims in tighter and tighter circles to evade capture. When the orcas killed Angela, she swam in the same pattern—having learned from dominating herself a method of surviving it.

What if the sharks had stayed? What if the sharks, despite the terrifying new reality of a creature bigger than them sharing their waters, eating their friends, tearing out their livers, etc., had decided to stay, to wait out the threat, to confront it? Scientists don't know where white sharks go to breed or how they give birth. They don't know much about how they parent. I imagine the number of sharks in the islands growing instead of shrinking, nearly coloring the surface of the water. The sharks continue their lives, deep and far below where we can see or even track them.

The Farallons are special because when white sharks surface there, it's shallow enough we can track their movements. When they leave to migrate, to make it to whatever mythical breeding ground they occupy some thousands of miles away, they dive so deep into the ocean that even the long-term, surgically implanted tags don't work anymore. The map goes dark, the red dots sputter and fade away, an expected disappearance.

Erin is watching me. I can feel it. I tuck my head back into the car, roll the window up, blow warm air into my hands. There's no polish on my nails anymore. My fingers are covered in scratches. When I climbed into the car, Erin immediately rolled down the windows. I still smell.

I never liked that someone could look at me and only see Erin. At Blake's funeral, a woman Erin used to work with pulled me aside and hugged me before I could get my arms up, she squished me, pinning my elbows against my sides. "I'm glad you still have your birth mom," she whispered. "It's a special connection."

Now I have Blake's face water-sealed across mine. No one can argue it anymore.

We pass the Berkeley Rose Garden, a coliseum of flowers, and our necks slide back as we hit the steepest patch of Marin, the rollercoaster's climb. We flatten out again as we turn onto our street, and then the house comes into view, our house with wooden stairs and a large glass window in front, no clock like Blake's childhood house had, but more of a view. We're either surrounded by fog up here or hanging just above it.

The mysterious building I saw at North Landing was called a blind, a structure designed to shield the observer from being seen while watching animals. I never saw it used.

I don't look at the house, with Blake's disappearance locked into the carpentry. I go inside, where the sharks swim back, where maybe they haven't even left in the first place, where they knew to stay and stayed.

# ACKNOWLEDGEMENTS

Thank you to everyone who dreamed into the book and into me, who made it possible to write, who kept me curious and flexible. I'm grateful, so always grateful.

Dear friends read drafts and sections of this book, showing me what I couldn't see—Jackson, Lizzy, as well as all the writers in my writers' group. Caitlin taught me about marine biology and where to look to learn more.

Lizzy leant me Karen Barad's *Meeting the Universe Halfway*; without it, there'd be no brittle star. Karen Barad's feminist vision of physics and matter-making inspired many of the thoughts that began this book.

Adam Rosenblatt fielded all my science questions and read my book with the utmost care as a biologist. Thank you, too, for the philosophical conversations about human and marine life and loss.

Ben and David took me on as a screenwriter from this book's sample. Thank you for connecting me with Alan, for pushing my work further, for standing up for me.

Kai had language underneath the words. Thank you for believing in punctuation as its own logic. For pauses. For less explanation, more feeling. For family and community in writing.

Emily was there for all the middle. Thank you for our pages exchange and for your quick, insightful, and believing eyes. For writing about the body and the inside, for inspiring me.

Nicole told me this short story should be a book. Thank you for our ongoing conversation on grief and absence. For speaking my language, for adding to it evermore.

Jaquén went through my drafts page by page. Thank you for sharing your sharp mind and huge heart with me. For modeling what it can mean to really show up for your work.

Elena found value in my messy narratives about my own high school life when we were sixteen, a first reader. Thank you for your forever friendship, and for pushing me to always keep going.

Andrea B. taught me how to celebrate the process, not the results, how it feels, not how it looks. Thank you for doing so with me.

Justin Taylor saw what was important in early drafts and encouraged me to follow it through—to write into the body and to leave only the right questions. Thank you for telling me about Great Place Books and urging me to submit the book to Alex and Emily. You're a true mentor.

My editors Alex Higley and Emily Adrian pushed me and the book to its best version. Thank you for finding the emotional truth in how one prepares an egg. For trusting me and helping me trust myself. Thank you to you both and Monika Woods for making a space for books like mine.

Aidan Fitzgerald designed how this book looks and feels, from the cover to the waves that begin each chapter. Thank you for your hard work and creativity in continuing the book in its design. It's more than I could have dreamed of. Mina Manchester was my thoughtful and thorough copyeditor; she made my sentences cleaner and meaner.

Brandon Malone took my author photo. Thank you for spending that sunny day in my neighborhood with me.

Nancy Steele, my former poetry teacher and current friend, gave me a grammatical view of the book, showing me all my strange choices with commas so I could decide I wanted to keep them that way. Far before there was a draft, a conversation at your house began the book. I'm grateful for your excitement at finding the Farallons in your binoculars on a clear day, perched on an upper level of the Lawrence Hall of Science parking lot.

My sister Olivia makes me laugh and makes my characters brave. My mom Audrey always believes in me as a writer, no matter how strange the path.

My mom Dawn continues to love me after she died. I find you in a calm body of water, in a cloudy piece of sea glass, in a wrinkled box of Milk Duds. It's surreal that you're not around for this, but of course you are.

Marissa loves me so well. You make me softer and stronger. You made it easier to write this book and finish it, and sometimes I think of your photographs to help me write landscapes with care.

Steven Jay Parcells told me a thrilling story about his science over tea at Nancy's house. Thank you for your spirit, for making me want to write about a scientist who loves water.

To end, I have to thank Lydia, the character that has lived with me for years now. I still think about where you'll end up. I love you and I wish you the most pleasant of surprises. I hope you won't forget the water, even though some of it hurt you.

Great Place Books publishes literary fiction, nonfiction, poetry, and work in translation. Our mission is to be a home for rigorous, weird, beautiful books—and their readers. These books are imperiled by the stratification and commercialization of publishing. Against the grain of the industry and the times, we aim to support the careers of idiosyncratic and alluring writers whose voices might otherwise be lost.

*www.greatplacebooks.com*